Just

One

Year

By

Lainy J. Thomas

Acknowledgments:

Thank you to my boys and girls who have supported me on this

journey, especially Nicky and Lucy for proof reading.

"Just One Year" has been professionally type set by Reedsy.com

Preface

On the eighteenth of March 2020, Prime Minister Boris Johnson announced that schools across the UK would close to all pupils except those of key workers as the coronavirus death toll reached one hundred and four within a matter of days. There had been widespread controversy and speculation prior to the announcement, with school children excited at the prospect of an extended Easter break and parents worried about childcare implications. Teachers, not quite believing it could happen, nevertheless were forced to plan for an unknown period of online learning – unchartered territory for all but the most tech savvy of schools. Everyone had an opinion about what was ahead but many scoffed loftily at the idea of the virus, quite rightfully quoting annual deaths from the flu as far out-weighing the, as yet, low number of fatalities from "Covid 19". Researchers and experts, however, warned that UK deaths could amount to 25,000 people if draconian measures were not urgently implemented. No one really believed this but, less than a week later, the country went into what would subsequently be dubbed as "the first lockdown" and dutifully, most people, in the ensuing weeks, stepped into an orderly acquiescence of the rules which shut down pubs, cafes, restaurants, theatres, cinemas, bowling alleys , hairdressers and beauty salons, gyms and swimming pools and all but essential shops. The great British queue came into its own and people stood quietly, two metres apart, to await their turn to enter the supermarket, hoping that there would have been a delivery of toilet roll and hand wash, which had been the first products to become the object of wide-spread panic purchasing. Hand sanitising and anti-bac spray routines prior to handling baskets and shopping trolleys quickly became second nature and face masks, initially a necessary evil, soon became the latest fashion must have co-ordinate.

Over the following weeks, that slid into months, families were forced to spend time together as the word "furlough" was introduced to their vocabulary and its mental, physical and fiscal impact gradually gnawed at the nation's well-being. Jobs were lost, companies closed down, some for good, whilst those who were lucky enough to gain from the months of being unable to spend their disposable income created an unprecedented boom in the demand for couriers as online shopping became the norm across the generations.

By the summer of that year, as "the first lockdown" began to ease, each family had its own story to tell. Even the strongest of marriages was bound to be tested as couples were forced to spend more time than ever together, time to discover their hitherto unobserved, annoying habits, time to discover their differences, time to idly succumb to internet searches. Other couples would discover their strength in the face of adversity whilst those with children were to find themselves teetering on the edge of control, navigating a global mental health crisis that was likely to impact for decades to come. By the end of December 2020, the official UK death toll had reached over 75,000, with the new year, seeing the whole country again in lockdown.

Chapter One

June 2020

"Mom ... Mom ....." Hannah's voice rose an octave in exasperation and there was an extra syllable thrown in for good measure, "Are you even listening to me?"

Josie brought her daughter's face back into focus, "Sorry, darling, yes ... erm, what did you say?"

"Doesn't matter, I'll walk." Hannah stared deliberately at the window where the rain was beating down noisily and relentlessly.

Josie backtracked and realised that Hannah had been asking for a lift to the train station. It was the first time that she had been anywhere for months but now that groups of up to six could meet up, she had arranged to meet a friend for a walk in a Birmingham park.

"It's fine, of course, I can take you. What time do you need to leave?"

Hannah sighed and grunted "ten minutes, if it's not too much trouble."

Josie opened her mouth and closed it again. She had long learned to choose her battles carefully and anyway, what did it matter? Her mind began to wander again. She wanted to be remembered as a good mom, the sort of mom who was there for you and didn't pick fights. She wanted to be remembered as kind, thoughtful, generous, funny, clever, loyal ... She felt a tear edge dangerously close and she poked at the corner of her eye.

"Mom, for god's sake! What's the matter with you?"

Josie arranged her face into what she hoped was a bright and apologetic smile. "I'm sorry, love, it must be my age ... hormones ... you know."

Hannah's face said "gross" and she rolled her eyes. "Great, thanks for sharing"

Fifteen minutes later Josie was saying a hurried goodbye whilst Hannah wrestled with her umbrella as she got out of the car, "Be careful! Keep me posted and let me know when you want picking up, I don't think this rain is going to stop and don't forget to wear your mask! Love you!"

"Bye mom"

No "love you too", Josie noticed and in the sanctuary of her car and alone, she allowed the tears to fall. Where had her life gone? Was this really it? Parked at the train station car park, just minutes from home, Josie turned off the engine and allowed her thoughts to wander to what she had found out the previous day. She had just one year to live.

Two days ago she had celebrated her 49th birthday and had had a quiet but lovely meal with her husband, Trevor, and their two children, who were not children. Harry was twenty one and Hannah just eighteen - another, newly fledged adult. They had all had their birthdays in "lockdown" and so gifts this year had been fairly constrained all round. They still had so many unused vouchers as well as postponed events and trips so there was no point buying more until the Covid nightmare was over. However, Trevor's birthday present had set her off on a downward spiral of self-pity and fury. How could she be married to someone who had bought her a bloody vacuum cleaner? She remembered his proud face as she tore the final piece of wrapping paper to reveal "the best robo vacuum cleaner 2020". What the hell? Really? Was that how dull she had become?

Her phone beeped, bringing her back to the present. It was Maria, her best friend since primary school, who had had a mini kitchen emergency and had not been able to bring her present on her birthday. The current Covid rules meant that visiting people inside their homes was not yet considered safe and they had optimistically pencilled in an afternoon in the garden drinking prosecco and reminiscing/putting the world to rights.

"Weather looking dodgy ... what do you think?"

Josie thought that if she didn't have some like-minded company soon, she would go completely insane. "We could sit in the conservatory and open all the windows .... "

They were both aware that those who were not deliberately flouting all the Covid rules and recklessly putting everyone else at risk, were trying to implement their own versions of social distancing. Three months of complete lockdown had taken its toll. People needed people. Josie needed to see her friend, even though she had sworn that she would tell no one her devastating news. This would be her burden and when she was gone they would have nothing but respect for the fact that she hadn't troubled them or dragged them down with her. One year to be whoever she wanted to be remembered as. One year to cram in the rest of her life.

Maria brought prosecco and flowers and beautiful treats, bath salts that smelled divine, indulgent body butter and candles that promised that she could create her own spa experience in the comfort (and safety) of her own home. They sat at what they considered to be a socially acceptable distance and gradually the rain slowed so they were able to open the door.

"Who would ever have imagined something like this? I still keep feeling shocked at the whole situation."

"Tell me about it, If I don't have a break from Trevor soon, I'm going to suffocate him, I swear!"

"Aww really? Actually, Mark and I have been getting on great considering we've never spent this much time together EVER!"

Mark was Maria's second husband and there had been a fair few other short-lived and disastrous liaisons but they were now on their sixth year of happy ever after and finally Maria appeared contented with their blended family of two boys and two girls between them.

"AND! I have some news!" Maria announced excitedly, topping up their prosecco glasses.

"Here's to …. me becoming a grandmother!"

"No way! Oh my god, that's amazing! Who? When?"

Maria could hardly contain her excitement, "Molly and Dan. Not planned but they are ecstatic"

Molly was Mark's eldest so technically, thought Josie, she wasn't actually going to be a grandmother. "That's fantastic, you better start knitting!"

"Shopping more like" quipped Maria. "I've already made an impressive start with Boots online. Look at this, she scrolled down her phone to show off her purchases that the screen assured her had already been despatched."

"They're gorgeous Maria. I am so envious."

What? Envious of her getting ready to being called granny? Who was she kidding?

"I haven't actually set foot in a shop yet since all this, have you?" Josie realised guiltily that she was changing the subject. She couldn't bear the pounding in her heart that reminded her that she had none of this to look forward to. She wouldn't get to see her children settle with the love of their lives and have successful careers, children ...

Maria gave her a strange look. "So how are your two? Sometimes I can't believe we have adults for children? Where did the time go? I was remembering the other day some of the funniest things that the kids did. Do you remember that time I treated myself to a trip to the beautician's and foolishly took Matt with me when he had just started talking and doing that thing where they say everything they are thinking?"

Josie sniffed, remembering Hannah, who at 18 still appeared to be at that stage when it came to telling her mother what an idiot she was.

Maria took another sip of her prosecco and giggled. "Oh my life, I nearly died of embarrassment. We were sitting in this waiting room, all calm and tranquil, Enya playing in the background, a beautiful water feature trickling tranquilly and Matt suddenly blurted, really loudly, "Mommy, what's that big fat man doing?"

Josie's eyes widened even though she'd heard this story many times.

"Well," continued Maria, "me being the naive fool of a mother that I was, I completely ignored him so he asked again, but this time, he'd made a more thorough inspection and concluded that it was a big fat lady. Dear god, the big fat lady was not impressed."

Josie laughed and reached for the tempting looking truffles that Maria had brought along. What did it matter if *she* got fat now? Would anyone even notice or care? She had always imagined that finally, in her very latter years, maybe around the age of eighty nine or so, she would eventually stop pinching her waist every morning to check her weight and would just give in to the heavenly temptation of all that she had resisted for so long.

"Are you ok?" Maria leaned forward, concerned. She was such a good friend, Josie reflected. Here she was, being a total bitch and hardly even acknowledging her exciting news but still Maria was concerned that she was not quite herself.

Once again, a large, salty tear escaped before Josie could catch it. Maria leapt out of her seat in horror and then checked herself. "For god's sake, this bloody virus, I can't even hug you. What on earth's the matter? What's happened? Tell me!" There was not much that they had not shared (and that was a whole other story) but Josie had promised herself that no one would know this horrible, horrible thing that she had discovered.

"I'm sorry, ignore me" Josie sniffed noisily", "hormones!"

"Tell me about it, Mark is a saint at the moment putting up with me"

Chapter Two

"Hi mom." Harry breezed into the kitchen. The Covid rules now meant that he could meet up for a walk with his girlfriend, Erin. They had been friends for ever and no one was surprised when they eventually became a couple, even going to the same university. They had both returned early with the Covid crisis forcing them to complete their studies remotely. They had been house-sharing with other students for the past two years but as neither of their family homes could comfortably accommodate an extra body, they had been forced to live separately during the pandemic. Now, they could at least go for a socially distanced walk but it was typical that after weeks of beautiful weather, the weather had now turned unpredictable and decidedly grim.

"Oh Harry, you're all wet!" Josie went towards her son, who laughed good-naturedly.

"Mom, I'm fine, stop worrying!" Harry was tall, slim and good looking with dark hair and deep brown eyes but he appeared to be completely unaware of how he turned heads. He was serious but funny and kind and Josie adored him. She was secretly pleased that one of the few bonuses of the current crisis was that her son had returned early to the family home. He had just completed his degree in English literature but had little idea of what he was going to do with it. He had toyed with the idea of doing a PGCE but the Covid crisis had meant that he had had plenty of time on his hands to reflect on his future.

Harry shrugged off his wet coat and moved towards the kettle. "Fancy a cuppa?"

"Of course, thank you." Josie pulled out a stool and settled herself at the kitchen counter. "How's Erin?"

"Yeah, she's good, you know Erin, nothing fazes her. She's applied to do her masters."

"Wow, that's amazing, you're all so clever." Josie pushed away the nagging voice that threatened to invade her moment of peace.

"Hey, son, where's mine?" Trevor came into the kitchen, paintbrush in hand. He had made the most of his lockdown furlough and was currently on room three of his project.

"Sorry, dad", Harry turned round and swiftly grabbed a third mug. "Hey, dad, have you heard that a cat has contracted Covid?"

"No w..."

"Yeah," interjected Harry, "Don't ask meow!".

"Idiot!"

Harry sat opposite his parents and Josie's stomach clenched as she realised he had an even more serious expression on his face than usual. Since the terrible discovery she had made, she had an almost permanent sense of dread that had taken residence in her belly and some sixth sense told her that what Harry was about to say was not going to make her feel any better.

"I need to tell you something." Harry reached over and touched his mother's hand and her eyes met his.

"Erin's not expecting my first grandchild is she?" Trevor said with a nervous laugh.

"Don't be ridiculous Trev, they haven't seen each other properly for months."

"Where there's a will, there's a way" chuckled Trevor.

Harry cleared his throat and Josie observed a gentle blush creeping up his neck. "I've got an interview tomorrow!"

"That's great, love, for what? Where?" Josie was already picturing him a working man, suited and booted, coming home every night for his tea.

Harry spoke quickly, eager to dispel any false ideas. "The interview's online".

"Oh yes, of course."

"The job's in Dubai."

Chapter Three

Josie lay next to Trevor, listening to his steady snoring. She prodded him and attempted to roll him on to his side but to no avail. It was no good, there was absolutely no way that she was going to sleep tonight. The past four months had been surreal, for everyone, not just her, she knew that. But right now she felt as though her whole world was falling apart. She had one year left, maybe less if she lost her mobility or became debilitated towards the end, who knew? She had not had much time to imagine how that year would be; everything was so uncertain, with all the talk of a second wave of the virus and the potential of a return to lockdown, the uncertainty of the employment situation, the housing situation, everything was up in the air. But the only certainty appeared to be that Harry was leaving. She hated herself as she realised that she was pinning all her hopes on him not getting the job, wanting her son to fail – what type of a mother was she? She remembered her confusion and the conversation earlier as Harry had tried to explain how he felt.

"This virus has made me realise, mom, that life is short,"

Josie had felt her chest constrict but had said nothing, she had just stared at her son and shoved Trevor's arm away unkindly, feeling inexplicably angry with him as if he had planted the idea in their son's head, which she knew he had not.

"You have to seize the moment, live for today and take everything that life has to offer." Harry had continued passionately, his brown eyes gleaming brightly. "I don't want to stay round here for ever and I don't just want to experience life in England. It's not like I'm saying I won't ever come back. The contract is just one year to begin with."

"Just one year." Josie had echoed, her voice dull and lifeless.

"Come on, Jose," Trevor had attempted to sound positive but Josie cut him off.

"What do you care?" she had shouted and then burst into tears as she saw the expression on Harry's face. This was a total nightmare. Is this how he was going to remember her? A selfish, stupid middle-aged woman who was scared to let him go, to spread his wings, to live the life she had given him?

"I'm so sorry, Harry. Please forgive me."

She glanced at her husband, "Sorry," she ventured sheepishly." "Everything has just got on top of me lately." She had taken a sip of her tea and turned back towards her son, attempting a smile. "Tell us all about it."

So Harry had explained that he was applying for a job as a teaching assistant in Dubai. If he was successful and subject to background checks, he would be gone within a couple of weeks, ready for the new term at the end of August.

"But what about Erin?" Josie had faltered. This was not at all how she imagined they were going to be living their lives.

Harry smiled his lovely smile and in spite of the words that followed, Josie could see how much he cared about the girl who had been by his side throughout his teenage years and into manhood. "Mom, we're young. We have the rest of our lives ahead of us. It would be foolish to settle down until … before …. well … before we've lived a bit."

"But how does she feel about it?" Josie asked, trying to keep her tone conciliatory.

"Erin's really supportive, as I would be of her. I'm not even going that far in the grand scheme of things, it's not like I'm going to Australia. Anyway, she can come out for a holiday. You all can. Think of the sun tans."

"Hmmph, don't the women have to cover up and be seen and not heard or something? Knowing my luck, I'd end up in jail." She heard the negativity in her voice and hated herself for it but somehow the words and the bitterness just kept tumbling out, her mind racing irrationally to thoughts of ending her life being mal-treated in an over-crowded and squalid cell.

As she recalled the conversation now, the tears began to fall. She crept into the en-suite. Trevor's snoring was even louder and she screamed silently as she peered at her reflection. Her hair, along with the rest of the nation's had not been cut in months and the spray on root concealer left her hair dull and matted but she wasn't yet ready to reveal her grey roots to the world. She looked exhausted and the sight made her cry even more. She splashed cold water on her face and reached for the magic eye cream that promised to reduce puffiness and dark circles. Josie crept downstairs and made her way to the kitchen, intending to make a herbal tea to help her sleep. She sat at the counter and raised the lid of her laptop. Harry had insisted on showing her pictures of where he would be working if he got the job, as well as some of the nearby hotels, which he assured her they could easily afford to book. "There's going to be loads of good holiday deals post covid, mom."

Hannah had walked in at that point and upon being brought up to speed with Harry's plans she immediately seized upon the opportunity to ask if she could have his room, which was quite a lot bigger than hers and she hadn't been happy that she had not been allowed to appropriate it whilst he was at uni.

"But Hannah," Trevor had reasoned, "You're going to be going to uni now, so you won't need to swap."

Hannah had not bothered to argue as she allowed her attention to be drawn to the pictures of the five star hotel that Harry currently had open on the screen. "Oh yes," she announced triumphantly, "I can definitely see myself sipping cocktails, on a lounger in the bikini I've not had chance to wear this summer!"

Harry had looked alarmed, "Maybe it will be Hannah that gets sent to jail mom, not you!"

Josie clicked off the website and turned her attention to Facebook. She had not bothered in recent weeks. What on earth was there to report? Nobody was going anywhere and no one had anything interesting to say. The Covid inspirational/funny videos that had been in abundance in the early weeks had dried up and she really didn't need to see photographs of what people were having for their dinner. She was surprised to see a "friend request" and her stomach did a quick somersault at the unexpected blast from the past.

Chapter Four

July 2005 – fifteen years earlier

Josie sat opposite her colleague, Jeff, and felt the sexual chemistry between them so strongly she was convinced that others would notice. She turned her attention to what he was saying, what he was asking.

"Come away with me Josie, just one night. I want you so badly, I can't stop thinking about you."

She was so so tempted, she wanted him too, more than she had ever wanted anyone. Why had she never felt like this about Trevor? Or had she? She honestly couldn't remember. They had been together since Josie was twenty and Trevor was just two years older. They had been part of a group of friends who had gradually all become couples. She couldn't recall any defining moment when he had walked into her life and set her heart racing. Now that they were in their mid thirties, had two children and full time jobs, they rarely had the time, let alone the energy for sex and certainly not for romance.

So she had set the plan in motion. She had confided in Maria who, in spite of her misgivings and her pleas to talk to Trev and re-kindle their marital passion rather than embark upon what would undoubtedly be a disastrous and painful mistake, had reluctantly agreed to cover for her. As far as Trevor was concerned, they were going for a girly spa day and an overnight stay so that they could both enjoy wine and dinner. He had been enthusiastic in his agreement that she deserved a break from the kids and Josie had astounded herself with the distinct lack of guilt she felt as she fantasised about her night of passion with Jeff. She secretly bought new underwear and massage oil and was crazy with desire as their date approached. They had been for a few drinks together after work when they had flirted outrageously but so far they had not succumbed to the temptation to even share a proper kiss and the prospect of being in his arms, feeling noticed and wanted was almost physically unbearable.

The day arrived and the plan was playing out to perfection with Josie having a leisurely shower whilst Trevor got the kids dressed and ready for a trip to the park. As she stepped out of the en suite shower room, however, she could hear the distinct wail of Hannah calling for her mommy. Hannah had always been a wilful and independent child but one who from birth was happy in her own skin and so the sound of her crying almost inconsolably stopped Josie in her tracks. She found Trevor, desperately trying to calm the young child, whilst holding a face cloth to her forehead.

"What's happened?" Josie's heart had lurched. "Has she fallen over?"

Trevor turned, his face set to a grim smile. "Chicken pox, love, her tummy's covered."

"Oh no, Hannah, sweetheart." Josie rushed to her side, crouching next to the bed where Trevor still sat, trying to cool her temperature.

"Don't go out, mommy, please stay with me. It hurts." Hannah launched into a fresh round of wailing.

Trevor spoke before Josie could react. "Hannah, don't worry, mommy will be back tomorrow. I'm here and Harry's here, we'll have some fun. When the medicine starts to work, you'll feel better. Mommy needs a rest."

Josie had glanced at the empty Calpol sachet and saw that he really did have things under control. It was not as though they hadn't been through it all before. Harry had had chicken pox at the same age; it had been so stressful as Josie had been in the late stages of pregnancy with Hannah. Now, at least, they didn't have that worry and hopefully Harry was now immune so he would be able to help keep his little sister occupied whilst she was gone.

She thought of Jeff and their plans for the day and evening and her pulse quickened. She wanted this so much. She deserved it, she told herself. Wasn't it about time she had some fun and a bit of goddam attention? She was sick of the drudgery of her life. Some days she felt more like a fifty year old with the total lack of spark in her life. Jeff made her feel alive, desired. He laughed at her jokes and noticed when she wore something new or tried out a new lipstick. They didn't just talk about the kids or what to have for dinner or what day the bins were due to be emptied, which pretty much summed up her conversations with Trevor.

"You go, love," Trevor had said quietly, "honestly, we'll be fine. You deserve a break and Maria will be so disappointed. You'll probably lose your money too."

Josie smiled at his pragmatism. He wouldn't mind her losing her money if he knew what she was planning to throw away instead. So in that moment, Josie had realised that she was incapable of the deception. Trevor was boring but he loved her and this was her family. She held Hannah's hand. "Don't worry, darling, mommy's not going anywhere. Let me just go and tell Maria, she'll understand."

Jeff had not forgiven her. He told her she was a "prick teaser" and then ignored her for weeks before obtaining a transfer to their partner company in the next town. Maria had told her it was for the best and encouraged her to "spice up her life" with her own husband instead of risking her marriage for the sake of a meaningless fling. Josie had told herself that what she felt for Jeff was not meaningless. She felt a connection with him and he brought out a side of her that she hadn't known existed. She felt adventurous, passionate, sexy and frivolous when she was with him and with Trevor she felt dull, predictable and undesirable.

However, after Hannah got over chicken pox, Trevor had surprised Josie with a night away that he had booked in secret. He had arranged for his mom to stay over – a rare treat as his mom was of the mindset that she had brought up her kids, she didn't need to start over with her son's. Josie remembered sadly that what had been an unprecedented and spontaneous gesture resulted in a series of events that led Josie down a path of sadness and self-loathing that never seemed to have completely left her.

She had had to admit that they had had fun. They had taken a boat trip in Stratford-upon-Avon and then had a leisurely lunch alfresco at a stylish bistro. They had laughed, mainly about the funny things that their kids said and did but they had relaxed in each other's company and as far as she could recall had had a not too dispassionate encounter on the hotel's enormous bed before falling asleep, more contented than she had been in a long time.

For a while, life seemed to take a more positive turn and Josie worked hard to push thoughts of Jeff from her mind. She threw herself into her work and enjoyed her family time with the children. She was fond of Trevor, loved him of course and knew deep down that she was doing the right thing by remaining faithful to her husband and loyal to her family. It was a few weeks later that, with a sense of horror and disbelief, Josie had discovered that she was pregnant and it was only with hindsight that she remembered that the unusually large amount of alcohol she had consumed during their night away had led to her throwing up violently in the early hours. They had laughed it off, glad that the kids were not around to witness the scene and after several pints of water, Josie had felt fine. She had not given a thought to the fact that, along with her fancy meal and vast quantities of sauvignon blanc, her body had also dispelled her contraceptive pill.

She recalled the conversation with Maria, in whom she had confided, without telling Trevor.

"I don't want this, Maria," she had wept, "I don't want to start all over again with breast feeding and nappies and sleepless nights. I can't do it. I love the kids I have but I don't want any more."

"It's your body, Josie, your choice." Maria had been so understanding and supportive. "It's the twenty first century for goodness sake. No one would blame you for taking control of your own life."

"But Trevor …" Josie had whispered, "He will want it, I know he will." She remembered that when Hannah had turned two, he had hinted that it was maybe time to start trying for baby number three and he had been shocked and upset that she had not shared his vision for extending their family.

"He doesn't have to know." Maria had said emphatically. "He's not the one who has to go through it all and let's face it, you will literally be the one left holding the baby. Two are hard enough work but three … and what about your career? You have said yourself how much you are enjoying work at the moment. What about your plans for promotion? I'm not saying it wouldn't be possible but we all know the reality of working mothers and their place on the ladder. If you do not want this pregnancy, you don't need to have it. Don't think of it as a baby, it's so early Josie. Hundreds of thousands of women take this decision, you shouldn't feel guilty."

Josie had wrestled with her conscience. She had always been convinced that she would never be one of those statistics. She had prided herself that she was in control of her life and didn't go around making such stupid mistakes. If only she had thought to take the morning after pill when she had been sick. What an idiot. The morning after pill was different wasn't it? That wasn't like an abortion. She shuddered at the word.

"Of course, it's the same thing!" Maria had protested when she had voiced her thoughts. "Josie, you are so early on, it's no different."

And so, knowing that there was no way that she wanted another child, Josie had made the appointment. She had just two weeks to wait until she could start to put this unfortunate incident behind her. She had not anticipated the unprecedented morning sickness that she suffered in the days that had ensued. Trevor, of course, had guessed. She feigned ignorance and innocence, passing it off as a tummy bug. But he had been insistent and had bought a pregnancy test. He waited, already turning over names and plans for their third baby whilst she peed on the stick with a sick sense of dread, knowing what the result would be and knowing how delighted he would be. She had sat on the toilet and stared at the result. He had hugged her and did a little dance around the bedroom.

"Oh Josie, I love you so much. This is going to be so great. You know, I always wanted three! This is fate, this baby is meant to be."

How on earth was she supposed to go through with the appointment to abort a child that was wanted so much by its father? Why, oh why was life so cruel? She thought of Amy, a colleague at work who was on her second round of IVF, battling against the odds and her own body clock, not to mention their budget, to conceive a child. She had cancelled the appointment and wept into her pillow.

Sometimes she wondered if there was a god and if so, how did he pick his sides? She didn't deserve for him to be looking out for her, but maybe he was. And if so, why wasn't he on Trevor's side? The side of the good man, the doting father? Why wasn't he on the side of the unborn baby, growing daily in her womb? Eleven and a half weeks into her pregnancy, she had stopped feeling sick and felt her energy returning. She recalled that she had cooked them a proper home cooked meal for the first time in weeks and Trevor had commented that she had regained some of her colour. That night as she got ready for bed, she spotted the tiny specks of blood in her pants and her heart leapt in horror. Her mind exploded into confusion. For the last few weeks she had sunk into an apathetic acceptance that she was going to have a third child. As with the previous two pregnancies, they had agreed that they would not make an announcement until the twelfth week and first scan so thankfully there had not been a whole load of baby talk to contend with. That night, she had slept fitfully and several times throughout the night crept out of bed to check. She had no idea whether the small amount of blood was indicative of the end of her pregnancy and she was even less sure of how she felt about it. She searched "spotting" silently on the internet and discovered that very often this was nothing to be concerned about. She had said nothing to Trevor but rang her doctor for advice. They advised her to go to bed and rest and normally the spotting would pass. How was she supposed to rest with two small children to look after, work and a house to run?

Two days later she painlessly felt the baby she had wanted rid of slip away. She saw the remnants: a bloody mess of discarded matter, the memory of which had never left her. She had once seen a tiny unborn chick that had fallen with its shell from a nest in their garden tree and it had looked the same. A tiny, precious, innocent being, that had taken its last breath before even its first. She had thought her heart would break and at the same time she was overwhelmed with a sense of relief that made her feel like the worst mother on earth. Trevor was bereft.

"We can try again, Jose." He had reassured her, "Lots of people go through this. We have just been so lucky that we have Harry and Hannah already."

He had stroked her arm tenderly and she was shocked with the venom with which she threw him off.

"We will *not* "try again"", she had spat. "I am never going through this again, Trevor." Her husband had no idea the extent of the "this" to which she was referring. The roller coaster of emotions, the guilt, the shame, the anger, the fear and finally a sorrowful relief.

Trevor loved her and would never hurt her. Josie knew that. She could call the shots and he might quietly disapprove and be disappointed but he would never turn against her. Josie was sterilised three months later.

Chapter Five

Josie's heart leapt now as she stared at the friend request. Jeff's name in front of her brought back a surge of emotions as she re-lived the events of fifteen years ago and she was temporarily frozen, her senses raging as she remembered the sight of him, the smell of him, the way he had made her ache with longing. Her thoughts returned to the present day and she reflected sadly on how lonely she felt at the prospect of her daughter leaving for uni and her son leaving for Dubai. Months of being cooped up due to Corona and all the plans for the summer discarded, leaving …. leaving what? What did she have to look forward to? Old age? Josie allowed herself a derisory laugh. Not even old age. Josie clicked "accept". Immediately, she logged out, terrified of what she had begun. Again. She told herself she was being ridiculous; he was just bored the same as everybody else in the country and was just being friendly. She crept back to bed and prepared herself for the sleepless hours that lay ahead. It was only later that she learned that at some point she must have fallen into a deep sleep.

Morning came and, half dozing, Josie began to think about another day ahead under "the new normal". Josie was working at home whilst Trevor was "furloughed" and much as Josie had tried to retain a routine, it was getting harder and harder not to hit the snooze button and force herself to get up at a regular time. Josie had not heard Trevor get out of bed but she heard him thundering back up the stairs and burst through the door. With a jolt, she recalled accepting Jeff's friend request. Her mind raced, had she done anything else? Had she closed down the laptop properly? What had Trevor seen that had set him racing up the stairs, shouting her name?

He burst into their bedroom, visibly shaken. She sat and faced him, voiceless.

"We've been burgled"

It was the last thing that she had expected to hear. For a solitary second, she felt relief that she had not been caught out and then the shock of what he had just said hit her like a thunderbolt. It was something she had always dreaded, having their homes invaded, violated. She had always felt astonished that people could sound so blasé when they spoke about it happening to them. She sprang out of bed.

"I don't understand why the alarm didn't go off" Trevor was muttering as he picked up his mobile to phone the police.

Josie felt her face redden. "Oh my god, I am so sorry, I couldn't sleep, I got up and read for a bit downstairs, I didn't want to disturb you. Trev, it's my fault, I am so sorry." She began to cry and then remembered that he hadn't even told her what they had taken, what damage they had done.

As it happened, Josie found herself feeling perversely grateful to the considerate burglars who hadn't trashed her home. They had come for Trevor's Mercedes, his pride and joy, the one materialistic thing that Trevor ever cared for was his car. He had always been a car fanatic but in January this year he had finally taken the plunge and signed up for a new AMG Line C Class. Due to the months of lockdown, it had hardly been driven. The thieves had found the spare keys in one of the kitchen cupboards. They had been as quiet as mice, having gained entry by removing the lock from the side door that led directly from the drive where their cars were always parked. Josie looked around and saw the kitchen as if through a stranger's eyes. How did they feel when they saw their personal possessions – the fridge magnets that told the stories of their travels, the plaque on the wall that announced "Our family doesn't have to be perfect to be wonderful" or the one she had placed with irony above the washing machine that read "self service laundry, wash, dry, repeat."

The police were unable to attend due to the virus but they issued them a crime number and Trevor made contact with the insurance company who demanded photos and statements and said that nothing could be done for two weeks, after which time, they would consider the car irretrievable. Harry and Hannah had been calm at first and sat with her in their unlockable home, whilst Trevor managed to order a click and collect replacement lock from the local DIY store. She said a small prayer of thanks that she had married a man with practical skills. If a job needed doing, Trevor was your man. It was only later that night when they all prepared nervously for bed that the reality of having had intruders in their home hit them. Josie had wiped every surface with anti-bacterial spray, she had disinfected the floor and opened all the windows, desperate to get rid of any real or imagined traces of the scum that had dared to enter their home and take their hard-earned possession. That night, Josie lay awake listening to the regular snoring of her husband and the sounds that houses make that you become accustomed to but now that the sanctuary of their home had been compromised, it was hard not to feel startled by every creak. She wanted to leap out of bed every time she heard a car or a voice in the generally quiet streets outside. For the first time that day she allowed herself to remember the friend request and the fact that she had responded to it. She turned to look at her husband beside her and knowing that nothing short of an earthquake would rouse him now, she picked up her phone and logged into her Facebook account.

Chapter Six

4 July 2020

The long awaited day arrived when pubs, restaurants, hairdressers, cinemas and theme parks were allowed to open their doors for the first time since March. Strict social distancing rules were to be enforced but it felt as though life was starting to return to normal. Hannah had her job back at the local pub, where she was aiming to get in as many hours as possible in order to boost her bank balance before leaving for uni. Trevor had returned to work although he was now working split shifts along with the rest of his team. It was a Saturday morning and Josie awoke early to the sound of the birds and the distant wail of a cat. She had slept surprisingly deeply. She put it down to exhaustion. It felt as though the roller coaster of events and emotions that were defining 2020 was destined not to stop any time soon.

A day earlier, Josie had sat opposite her son as he read her the email. His application had been successful. He would be leaving in a few weeks to start a year long contract in Dubai. Part of her was proud of course but she was fearful, afraid of the unknown and of losing him for good.

"You're not losing me, mom." Harry had explained patiently and kindly. "We will skype every week at least. It's a great opportunity. Please be happy for me."

Josie had reached across to stroke his cheek, a manly stubble grazing her palm. "I am, son, I'm sorry. It's just that I worry … you'll always be my baby."

Harry's face took on a more serious look.

"What?" Josie knew that there was something else he had to say.

He took a breath and his face reddened. "I've split up with Erin." He let the words sink in.

"What?" Josie was not expecting this. The bombshell exploded in her mind. What was going on? Harry and Erin were … well they were Harry and Erin, they couldn't split up … could they?

"Why? Oh my god, Harry, I am so sorry, what on earth has happened? Are you ok? Is she ok?"

Harry smiled slightly. "Nothing has happened, mom. Calm down! She's fine. I'm fine. Everything's fine. Well I hope so." His voice tailed off.

"H… Harry, what do you mean, you're confusing me. You've split up but everything's fine " Josie was baffled.

"Mom." He put his hands to his mouth as if he didn't really want the words to come out. "Mom, I think I'm gay."

Josie stared at her son blankly.

"Say something please, mom." Harry suddenly sounded young, vulnerable and frightened. He didn't sound now like the confident young man that was telling her moments ago about his new adventure thousands of miles away.

"I'm sorry. Harry. I don't know what to say." How had she not seen this coming? What type of a mother was she that had failed to notice this? Had it been obvious? Did everyone else know? She put her head in her hands.

"Mom, please, you're frightening me. Please tell me it's ok? I'm still me, I'm still the same person. It's … it's not something I've chosen, it's just the way it is, the way I am. I have tried to be "normal", honestly, I have tried, with Erin. I love her but not in that way. I am just not attracted to girls." He was babbling now and Josie sat and looked at the anguish on his face.

She rushed round to his side and took him in her arms. He hugged her tightly and she felt the sobs rise as he gave in to a tide of emotion. Josie held her son, her beloved boy and she too began to cry.

"I'm so, so sorry, Harry." She held his head in her hands and looked at him fully, both of their faces tear-stained, "Of course, it's ok. It's ok!" She said firmly, "But I feel terrible, not to have realised. You must have been through hell" She looked at him searchingly but he shook his head.

"Don't worry. I mean … yes, I have been confused but…well Erin's been great, she has helped me understand … a lot."

"She's a great girl." Josie heard the tinge of sadness in her voice.

"She is." Harry agreed, "But I could never have made her completely happy. She will find someone else and we will be friends … always." He smiled at her and Josie wiped away her tears and shook herself.

"Anyway, what do you mean? Normal? There's no such thing as normal. I just want you to be happy and a good person. That's all I've ever wanted for both of you."

The relief in Harry's face was visible but then a cloud came across his eyes, "What about dad?"

"What do you mean?" But Josie suspected she knew what he meant. Trevor was old fashioned, not prejudiced exactly but there were some things he "couldn't get his head round." They both knew that he would not find it so easy to accept their son's announcement. "Leave it to me," Josie stated, "or, I mean, unless you want to talk to him yourself?" She did not want to wade in and take over, it was her son's decision.

"No," Harry's response was decisive and swift but then he ventured hesitantly "But, mom, I want you to wait until I've gone away."

Josie was not so sure that this was a good idea but Harry would not be swayed. "I know I'm being a coward but I just can't do it. Not yet. I'm only just coming to terms with it myself. I'll still be spending time with Erin. She's my best friend, mom, so dad probably won't even notice anything different, it's not like I'm getting it tattooed on my forehead or anything!"

Josie smiled, and breathed a silent breath of relief that her son was gentle and kind but not overtly camp or in your face gay, more of a Will Young than a Boy George, she reflected.

Chapter Seven

Josie had arranged to go round to Maria's for a glass of wine and a catch up. They still didn't feel comfortable going to indoor public places. There was so much conflicting information about the R rate and whether or not numbers of those infected with or dying of Covid 19 were decreasing. In the early days of lockdown, the police had been proactive in questioning those breaking the lockdown and had had no qualms in issuing fines but in the wake of members of the government having broken the rules and the months of frustration, many people seemed to be determined to live their lives normally, come what may. Reality appeared to have been suspended in the months since going into lockdown, the British prime minister had himself looked death in the face as he fought his own battle in intensive care with the previously unheard of virus. Schools had closed for the first time in living memory and pop up hospitals had been built to help alleviate the strain on the NHS. For three months, the only sense of socialisation came with the weekly clap for carers each Thursday at 8 p.m. when people took to their doorsteps in a show of solidarity for those on whom, it was now more widely acknowledged, their lives depended. But now, as life slowly returned to normal, lockdown was quickly forgotten by many and there had been shocking photographs of people failing to observe social distancing on crowded beaches and newly opened pubs and clubs. The scenes were looked at in horror by those such as Josie and Maria who were only too aware of their own and their families' vulnerabilities and were in no hurry to rush to mingle with the invisible, deadly virus.

Maria was looking tired as she welcomed Josie and wasted no time in pouring them each a generous measure of prosecco. They sat in the garden, which was in full summer bloom and the peaceful atmosphere was enhanced by the gentle trickle of the impressive water feature that resided in a corner, surrounded by a burst of geraniums. Josie and Maria were never short of conversation; they knew each other's family members, friends and colleagues, either in person or because they were spoken about so frequently. Surprisingly, in the current circumstances, they found plenty of things to talk about - everyone knew someone who had either had the virus, was shielding, furloughed or worse - had been made redundant. No one was coming out of this unscathed. Holidays had been cancelled and only the bravest were ploughing ahead with their plans or had made last minute bookings in an attempt to enjoy a break from the monotony and uncertainty of spring and summer 2020 and in pursuit of some guaranteed sunshine.

Josie was conscious that, for the first time ever, she seemed to be holding back from sharing with her friend the significant events that were currently threatening to overwhelm her. Somehow, she could not find the words or the energy to share the thoughts that kept her awake at night despite the fact that she felt sure she would go crazy if she didn't talk to someone soon. She worried about Harry's recent revelation that now seemed to define his future and as for the secret that Josie was keeping to herself, there was no way that she was going there. Even with her lips sealed on these events, they chatted endlessly and Maria was full of sympathy for Josie as she described their recent burglary experience.

Josie had made light of it even though the thought of strangers, intruders, criminals inside her house made her shudder with revulsion and fear at what might have been. What would have happened if one of them had disturbed them? What would have happened if they had not found the keys downstairs, would they have woken them in their beds? What would have happened if they had seen their beautiful daughter, practically naked as she slept? Or her handsome son? Why did she assume that the burglars were male or even heterosexual? We are all prejudiced in some way, she had realised. But now as she sipped her prosecco, she joked that she was grateful that the burglars had been so thoughtful as to have not made any mess and had even left the unfinished bottle of merlot on the side, untouched.

They laughed that the world seemed to have gone mad indeed.

"Hannah told me the other day," giggled Josie "that there's a rap star running for president in the US!

Good god, what next? The lunatics really have taken over the asylum!"

They reflected sadly on the events within the British royal family with Harry and Meghan no longer senior royals and rumours of the ongoing rift between the royal brothers.

"It's so sad, Diana would be heartbroken. I loved Princess Diana" mused Maria sorrowfully.

"Me too" agreed Josie. "I remember those two boys being born and I'll never forget the sight of them at their mother's funeral. It's a miracle they have turned out as they have and it makes my blood boil that the media are yet again ripping their lives apart."

"I know, me too." Maria was passionate in her support of the late princess. "I mean, she had her faults, what with her affairs and what not but let's face it, bloody Charles didn't exactly make it easy for her did he?"

They were well into their second bottle now and Josie suddenly felt brave enough to share news of her newly rekindled, albeit on-line, friendship. Her stomach turned over as she watched Maria's expression harden.

"Please don't tell me you are thinking about going down that route again?"

Josie was startled and slightly indignant. "Erm, I didn't actually ever go down that route, if you recall."

"Not for the want of trying." Maria muttered in a tone that Josie didn't recognise. Maria looked Josie in the eye and leaned forward, wine glass in hand as she pointed her finger accusingly.

"Your problem, Josie, is that you've never known which side your bread is buttered".

Josie felt her heckles rising. "And what exactly do you mean by that?"

"What I mean ... " Maria now placed her glass down with such force, she practically slammed it on to the table between them. "What I mean is that you have a husband who has always been devoted to you. You have two beautiful, clever children, a lovely house, a good job. Why don't you start appreciating what you have got instead of whinging about what you haven't? Bloody hell, even the burglars you had were kind to you. So what if they took the car! It's a car! They didn't kidnap your daughter ... or..... or worse and what the hell do you pay your insurance for anyway? You even said yourself that you had your excess insured. It's not like you have actually *lost out!*"

"Whinging?" protested Josie hotly. "How would you like it if someone came into your house whilst you were asleep?" Josie was outraged. "And anyway, who the hell are *you* to criticise me? So, you're telling me it's fine for you and Princess bloody Diana? You! You've had more affairs than I've had hot dinners."

Maria stood up, seething. "The big difference is, Josie …" Maria was red in the face by now and her hand shook as she stabbed her finger into the air for emphasis. "The big difference is …. I had a husband who abused me, belittled me, hit me … treated me like crap. That's the difference. So pardon me if I feel ever so slightly, a bit more bloody justified in my eventual lack of fidelity and for taking the chance to find happiness." She was breathless with outrage; Josie opened her mouth to speak but Maria did not give her chance. "And Princess bloody Diana didn't run it by me first so don't blame me for that!" She crossed her arms in front of her body. Her mouth a hard line. "I think you should leave now."

Chapter Eight

Maria sat alone in her garden and tears of frustration and anger rolled down her cheeks. How had that just happened? Josie was her best friend and she had handled things completely wrongly. Was it the consequence of the lockdown and the stress about the virus? Just lately she had been on a very short fuse. She reflected on what Josie had thrown at her "more affairs than I've had hot dinners." It was not exactly fair but it had hit a nerve. Maria had married her first husband at twenty two and they had had two children within four years. With hindsight and maturity, she had come to realise that Andy had always shown signs of being abusive. She had been swept away by his charm and when he told her what to wear, she had found it endearing that he took so much notice and wanted her to look nice. It was done so subtly that she didn't notice that eventually the clothes that he told her to choose were the ones he considered would gain her the least amount of attention. Over the years, he had chipped away at her self-confidence, he laughed at her opinions, made jokes about her if she dared to do something different with her hair or make up.

She remembered the time she had dressed in a new leotard and lycra aerobic pants to join a keep fit class that she and Josie had signed up for. She had been looking at herself in the mirror, trying to convince herself that she looked ok when he had come into the bedroom, laughed and told her she looked "fucking ridiculous." She had put on a baggy tee-shirt over the new outfit and later had told Josie that the class wasn't really her thing, giving it up the following week, before she had barely begun. And then came the physical violence; he was always so remorseful afterwards but as soon as she accepted his apology, he would lay the blame at her feet, telling her that she made him angry and that she shouldn't wind him up. Ultimately, it was never his fault.

Maria had had a disastrous fling with her boss. Disastrous because he, of course, was just using her for sex. He could see that she was vulnerable and like the leech that he was, sucked away at the last shreds of her self-esteem when he dumped her and sacked her, laughing at her when she threatened to take him to court because he knew that she would not, could not, go public with their affair. The final nail in Maria's coffin had been when her son, Matt, at eight, had started to mimic his father, speaking to her as though she were beneath him and mocking her in front of his little friends who in turn had copied him. Maria took the children and rented a flat, scrimping to make ends meet and having to take Andy to court before he paid his way. Maria had had, it was true to say, a number of meaningless affairs in the years before she met her second husband Mark. She had not been particular in checking whether the men she met on the internet were married and she woefully regretted her behaviour. Looking back, she knew that she had simply just been craving the attention that she had not had for so long. As soon as a man paid her a compliment, she was prepared to give herself away, telling herself that in this day and age, she was an independent woman, able to do as she pleased with her body. Ultimately though, her brief and loveless encounters were as damaging to her confidence as her abusive marriage. And then at last, fate must have decided to give her a break and Mark had walked into her life. He was the most open and honest man she had ever met. They had taken things very slowly at first and she was ashamed to say that she was not entirely honest with him in the beginning as she continued to see other men in between their occasional dates. However, one night, as she lay in his arms and he spoke tentatively of their future together, of their children meeting and family holidays they could take, she felt something fall into place in her heart. They set up home together six months later and married the following year. Everyone envied how well their children seemed to get along and finally it seemed that life was as perfect as it could be.

Maria, sitting now, reflecting on her argument with Josie, recalled how Josie had been there for her, through thick and thin. Josie had never disguised the fact that she had never really liked Andy but it was true to say that at the time Maria had not told her the extent of his abuse. She had never told anyone. It was her dirty secret, the fact that she had been so pathetic as to put up with his behaviour; the shame had never left her.

Nevertheless, it was Josie who had seen how unhappy she was, how she had become a shadow of the vivacious and funny teenager that she had been and Josie had given her the confidence to finally leave Andy, to take her children and make a life by herself. Josie had helped with babysitting; even though she had her own to look after, she had never minded having a houseful of children. Her children had grown up with Josie's and they were as close as cousins, siblings even.

2020 certainly was an "Annus horribilis" for the entire nation, practically the entire world. Few people had taken too much notice when the word "coronavirus" first appeared in the news. It was something going on in China, which was so far away and anyway didn't thousands of people die of the flu every year? What was the difference? But the virus gathered pace and the shock of the first recorded death in England eventually became a distant memory as the numbers reached tens of thousands who had lost their lives and hundreds of thousands of people having tested positive for the virus in the UK alone. Holidays had been cancelled and then re-scheduled but the uncertainty of a second wave, local lockdowns and quarantine rules were all creating chaos, not to mention the economic impact, which was destined to end in recession. Airlines, department stores, pubs and restaurants had made massive redundancies and many people were still "furloughed", unsure of whether or not they would have a job to go to at the end of it.

But for Maria and Mark, lockdown had brought a further blow. At the end of March, just days into "lockdown" Mark had received a phone call from his GP. He had been having twice yearly blood tests for the past few years. High blood pressure ran in his family but it was under control through daily medication and a reasonably healthy lifestyle. Following his last test, however, he had been sent to the hospital for a second blood test due to "high white blood cells". Maria and Mark of course had googled this immediately and had looked in horror as they discovered the range of explanations offered not so helpfully by the online medical websites. But then they had laughed it off, of course it would just be an infection, Mark couldn't possibly have leukaemia. He was too tanned, too strong …

But the nice doctor from the surgery had told them, in fact, that he did. Apparently, there were lots of different types of leukaemia and Mark had managed to develop the "best" type. The name "chronic lymphocytic leukaemia", didn't sound like anything good to Maria and Mark but as the doctor explained, it was a condition that meant that he would probably live a normal life and require no treatment. He would just be monitored. For ever. It was referred to as "watch and wait" but as Maria discovered, many sufferers and their families felt that it was "watch and worry". Her husband had blood cancer. And it was never, ever going away. They decided to tell no one. What was the point? Imagine telling people that you had cancer but there was no treatment. They would think you were making it up. It was absurd but thousands of people according to their now extensive research lived with this condition. There was no way of knowing when it might suddenly deteriorate and no way of knowing what the prognosis was. But as they started to come to terms with the shocking news, they realised that this was pretty much the same situation for everyone. No one knows how long they have, you just have to make the most of it. Covid 19 had brought this home to everyone so really they were no different to anyone else . At least, that's what they tried to convince themselves. So they avoided the C word but subscribed to "Blood Cancer UK", took comfort from their support during the pandemic and were determined to stick to their word that no one else needed to share their burden.

Inwardly, Maria, however, raged at the injustice. Finally, after all her years of unhappiness and loneliness, she had found Mark and imagined that they would grow old together. They talked about how they would spend their retirement, travelling and spending time with their children and what she imagined would be a brood of grandchildren. Now, she looked at her beloved husband and feared an old age of loneliness and believed that it would actually be possible for her to die of a broken heart. However, as much as she adored her husband and wanted to cherish every moment they had together, she knew that she was being short-tempered and her mood swings were obvious to those close to her. She apologised on an almost daily basis, blaming her age and her hormones and at night she wept silent tears and vowed that tomorrow she would wear her cheerful face and try to be the wife that Mark deserved.

And so it was that Maria and Josie, lifelong friends, came to verbal blows and stopped speaking, texting, whatsapping family pictures and Covid jokes. Their friendship, which they had both believed to be invincible, was stopped in its tracks, leaving each of them at a loss to know how it had happened or how to fix it. Each of them locked in by their own sorry secrets, each of them as stubborn as the other.

Chapter Nine

It was bizarre how the weeks and months had rolled by since March; weeks of lockdown, social distancing, daily briefings with incomprehensible graphs and phrases such as "The R Rate" being added to their vocabulary and the sight of people wearing masks becoming common place. Trevor had joked that Michael Jackson must be moon walking on a cloud, laughing his white socks off – they had all thought he was crazy but only the crazy would venture out with a naked face now. However, some semblance of normality was slowly returning, with many people returning to work and shops, hairdressers and gyms were open by the end of July. Josie, though, continued to feel that she was living on a knife edge. She scrutinised her face, her body for signs of the illness that would end her life prematurely. She was hyper-sensitive to every slight twinge or the merest suggestion of a headache. Logic told her that stress was exacerbating her condition but knowing this and being able to control it were two very different matters.

August arrived and the tension in the household seemed to increase daily. Hannah was on tenterhooks, waiting for the results of exams she had not sat. Harry was busy researching and preparing for his new role and in spite of his excitement, was understandably anxious about living in a foreign country with a very different culture. Even though he had been officially offered the job and had accepted, he had not been given a start date due to the uncertainty that surrounded travel and schools re-opening. Josie tried to give them both her support and attention but she was distracted. She missed her regular text conversations with Maria and she was bored by Trevor; having him around the house due to his shift working and her working from home was driving her insane. He had developed a tendency to tidy up, re-organising her chaotic cupboards with a sense of satisfaction that drove her mad. She enjoyed her organised chaos, she always found what she was looking for, it just looked chaotic to the untrained eye. Nowadays she would be in the middle of cooking and reach for the black pepper from where it normally nestled happily amongst the tinned vegetables, only to discover that it had now been neatly but practically invisibly re-homed amongst the herbs and spices that she hardly ever used. Made perfect sense to Trevor. Grrrr!

Josie's only reprieve from the humdrum existence of working from home, the drudgery of the housework, life with Trev and the worries about her health and their children's future, not to mention the responsibilities they felt towards their own quite elderly parents, was the now almost daily escape in the form of her on line chats with Jeff. They exchanged what she would consider "banter", each complaining about their spouses and ungrateful adult children. Josie learned that he too had two grown up children and he more than hinted at the fact that he was still with his wife for "practical purposes" and that they both pretty much lived their own lives. Lockdown with her, he complained, was pretty much like torture and it was clear that he would very much welcome someone spicing up his life after months of isolation. He was as suave as ever and made it clear that he didn't just want anyone to do the spicing up.

"I've never forgotten you Josie." He told her repeatedly during their on line chats. "You were always special, I was so attracted to you. I was heart-broken when we split up."

Josie had wondered vaguely at the reference to splitting up. Was he confusing her with someone else? But she was easy prey to his flattery and blushed like a schoolgirl in front of her laptop when he told her that she looked so much younger than her 49 years and that she had hardly changed a bit. "My wife has literally turned into her mother." He grumbled, "It's the stuff of nightmares. Now, you, Josie, my love are what dreams are made of."

He was sickly sweet and fake and deep down she knew it but it was better than being ignored, taken for granted. Better than being infuckingvisible!

Chapter Ten

As if to add emphasis to the chaos that Corona was wreaking around the world, the UK's weather became crazily unpredictable and August saw violent thunderstorms, torrential rain and soaring heat, interspersed with days that were sunny, cool, dull, windy or miserable but no two consecutive days were the same. One evening, Josie, Trevor and their two children had just finished their evening meal when the most horrendous storm erupted, with rain pouring from the sky and thunder crashing overhead. Unusually, they were all sat together in the living room, watching the storm, the lightning flashing menacingly and the thunder crashing angrily overhead.

Suddenly Harry sat bolt upright, gripping his phone.

"Oh my god, I had an email this morning, I didn't see it."

Josie felt her stomach tense and looked at Trevor who was watching his son.

"What?" Even Hannah was eager to know his news.

Harry chewed his lip and lifted his eyes to meet first his mother's and then his father's. " The job in Dubai! I start in three weeks!!"

A flash of lightning lit up the room and it seemed for Josie that time froze as she watched literally buckets of rain pour from the sky. The thunder cracked and ripped through Josie's heart. She was losing her son. He was going away from her, so far away and she might not be around when he returned.

Trevor was the first to break the heavy silence between them all. "That's fantastic news, son. At least you can start getting on with your life now."

"Yeah," offered Hannah, "nice one bro! Good on ya"

Josie felt a huge sob threatening to erupt and she felt as though she were being suffocated. For the past few weeks, she had refused to acknowledge to herself that Harry would actually go. So many things had been planned this year that had not actually come to fruition and in her mind she had started to believe that this would just become another cancelled plan.

"Come on mom," Harry's voice was soft, but she could tell that he was disappointed with her lack of enthusiasm and praise. "It's just one year! I'll be back before you know it and hopefully this bloody virus will be all over."

Josie sniffed noisily. "I know, I'm sorry, Harry." She made a huge effort to pull herself together. "I am proud of you, I really am. Ignore me, I'm just being pathetic."

Trevor held her tight that night in bed and kissed her shoulder tenderly. He was a man of few words but he tried to console her. "We have to let them live their lives, Jose", he whispered gently. "They're not children any longer. Remember what we were like at their age, the last people we spent time with was our parents. And anyway, he has Erin to come back to, so that's one guarantee that he'll be back."

He had no idea why this brought on a fresh round of tears. She had promised Harry that she would say nothing to his dad until he had left. She felt the weight of the secrets she was keeping heavy on her heart and knew that there would be no sleep tonight. She lay in the dark, listening to the now distant rumble of thunder. She didn't even feel tempted to lose herself in banter with Jeff. She felt so alone, so afraid and so utterly sad.

Chapter Eleven

Amid a furore of media speculation and criticism of the government's handling of exam results, the morning arrived when Hannah was due to collect her results. Students had been given specific, individual times so that there was limited social interaction and Hannah's time was 11.15. Her school was a fifteen minute's drive away and by 10.45 she was desperate to find out her fate. She had put on her trainers and was beginning to pace around the kitchen. Josie, who had just cleaned the tiled floor, couldn't help but pounce on her daughter; she had always hated germs on her floor even before the global pandemic.

"Hannah, stop walking on the floor." she snapped.

"For god's sake, mom what do you expect me to do, bloody hover?"

Josie had looked at her daughter, realising that in normal circumstances, this would have been comical.

"Come on, let's leave now, we'll get a drive through coffee on the way." Anything was better than being tortured by the thought of all those nasty germs being traipsed around her kitchen. Covid was driving her towards paranoia and the anti-bac spray had become an almost permanent extension to her arm.

Hannah sat silently in the car and Josie tried to reassure her that whatever happened, there were always choices and everything would turn out fine. She prayed that her daughter would get the results that she needed but at the same time, dreaded that in a few weeks' time, she would potentially have become an empty nester. Josie was so nervous that she completely mis-judged the distance when pulling up next to the kiosk at the drive-thru and had to actually get out of the car to receive the drinks being handed over.

"Jesus, mom, you're such an idiot! So embarrassing!"

Josie pushed away the feeling of incompetence; an embarrassing, middle aged, un-cool mother and instead made light of it "Not to worry, worse things happen at sea!" Inside she felt useless, unappreciated and stupid. It seemed like a lifetime ago since her children believed she was the font of all knowledge, beautiful, the person who made everything better.

Josie had to wait inside the car. Parents were classed as visitors and they were not allowed on the school site. She sat staring intently at the side mirror, watching her daughter exit the building and walk towards the car. Hannah's head was down and Josie's heart sank. No matter how they spoke to her sometimes, her children were her life and if they hurt, she hurt. "Please, Hannah, get your head up." She had spoken silently to herself. Earlier she had made Hannah promise not to "have her on" so as she studied the sight of her daughter, she believed that it must be bad news. Josie felt the beginnings of a sense of rage stirring inside her. This stupid virus and all the trouble it had caused. There was no way that her daughter should not get her predicted results, she had worked so hard, even during lockdown when many kids had given up.

Hannah burst back into the car and let out a scream.

"I did it! Mom! I did it! And I've had an email from Liverpool Uni ! I've got in. Mom, I've got in".

Josie felt her heart burst with pride and relief at the same time as a thousand butterflies invaded her stomach. Her daughter was a grown up, going to uni!

"I'm so pleased for you, Hannah." She hugged her daughter. "Durr!! I told you not to trick me! I'm so proud of you! " She quashed the voice in her head that reminded her that she would not be around to see her graduate and forced her voice to sound normal and elated. "Well done!"

And so, as the end of August approached, Josie prepared to wave goodbye to both of her children as they embarked upon their respective adventures. Josie went to great lengths to remain cheerful in front of the rest of the family and she noted with relief that Hannah and Harry were making a big effort to spend some time with her each day in spite of how busy they were, making plans and seeing friends that they would not be seeing for a while. The "Eat out to help out" scheme, initiated by the government in a bid to kick start the hospitality industry, which along with many other sectors had taken a massive hit from the enforced lockdown that had lasted way longer than anyone had imagined, meant that Hannah was rushed off her feet at the local pub. She invariably returned with some story about grumpy customers who complained that the "curry was too lumpy" or the "soup too thick" or some such triviality and one day she made Josie laugh with a story about an elderly lady who at the end of the meal confessed that she had mistaken the sachet of vinegar for a sachet of hand sanitiser and had rubbed it enthusiastically all over her hands before starting on her fish and chips.

"Please shoot me if I ever end up so stupid." Hannah had grumbled.

"You won't Hannah." Josie had smiled "But *I'm* probably well on the way to senility."

Or maybe not … said the voice in her head.

Chapter Twelve

Trevor and Harry were set to leave for the airport. The previous day they had all been out to lunch as a farewell celebration. Erin had come along and Trevor had jokingly questioned her about how she was going to survive a year without the love of her life. Erin had shifted awkwardly and looked across at Josie. Erin had built up a close relationship with Josie and Trevor over the years and she knew that Trevor would find it difficult to come to terms with his son's sexuality. He was a good man but old fashioned and had been brought up to believe that being gay was a sin; it was hardly surprising when you considered that up until 1967, homosexuality had been illegal in England and so for Trevor's parents and many of those of that generation, it was difficult to understand how something that had been considered criminal, was now to be treated as normal . Since Harry's revelation, Josie had had a heart to heart with Erin one day whilst Trevor was out playing golf. Erin had admitted that she had long since suspected that her boyfriend was gay, which, she confessed had messed her head up, but ultimately, she knew that her love for him meant that she had to let him go.

The tears had slid down her cheeks as she confessed "I know he loves me with all his heart. He would walk on hot coals for me, but he just doesn't love me in that way, you know?" Josie had nodded silently, knowing exactly what she meant. "I think he loves me like a sister and there's nothing I can do to change that." She had smiled forlornly. "I wouldn't want to change that because I want him to be happy and to be true to himself." She had added and Josie had felt her heart fill with love for the two of them, torn apart by an impossible love.

"He will be, love," Josie had reassured her. "And you will be too. It's probably for the best that there will be some distance between you." She tried to convince herself too that it was all going to be for the best and tried not to think about the fact that she wouldn't be around for her son's return. She would never know whether or not "it all worked out."

"Will you tell Trevor, once Harry's gone?" Erin had enquired, with a look of consternation on her face.

Josie had breathed a deep breath, thinking of the conversation she would need to have with her husband. It was not going to be easy. "I will have to," she had replied. "I promised Harry and well . . . he needs to know . . . we can't have Harry living a lie."

"I know." Erin had smiled hesitantly. "He will probably meet someone and he can't be expected to have a secret boyfriend can he?"

In spite of herself, Josie had started at the thought of her son having a boyfriend. She too needed some time for all of this to sink in. "How does that make you feel?" she had asked Erin tentatively. This was the man that they had all expected her to spend the rest of her life with…marry, have children with and now she faced the prospect that he would fall in love not just with someone else but with a man. How would she feel if she were in Erin's shoes? She laughed inwardly. The prospect of Trevor being gay was ridiculous. Wasn't it? Oh my god, she had suddenly had the most terrifying thought that maybe that was why he didn't seem interested in her physically. But it hadn't always been like that … had it …. Josie tried to remember the passion of their youth … had it been real? She felt as though she were drowning in quicksand, everything seemed to be slipping out of her control, her understanding. She forced herself to bring her thoughts and her attention back to the present as Erin answered her question.

"I feel …. jealous." Another tear had slid quietly down her cheek. "I feel sad … but also happy for him … like I said, I just want him to be happy." Josie reached out to hug the girl that she had thought would become her daughter-in-law, bear her grandchildren. She checked herself abruptly, they were still not allowed to hug people from different households.

"Damn this bloody virus to hell!" Josie had exclaimed and then reached out again and enveloped the girl in a tight hug, stroking her hair and whispered softly. "He has been so lucky to have had you in his life, Erin. I'm so sorry that he has let you down."

"He hasn't let me down." Erin had been quick to defend him. "It's not his fault. It's complicated. We were so close, it was natural for everyone to see us as girlfriend and boyfriend and I think he just kind of went along with it because …. I don't know … because it was probably easier. Even in this day and age, it's hard to … to "come out", especially if you are not an extrovert type of person."

"Humph!" Josie had objected "Come out! Flaming coming out! What's that all about?" She had given this some thought since her son had done just that. "People don't come out as being heterosexual do they? Can you imagine how that conversation would go …. Hey, guess what, I just discovered last night that I'm heterosexual?"

Erin had laughed. It was absurd. "No, you're right. It's actually quite preposterous. It's nobody's business."

"Absolutely," Josie endorsed, "People will only be truly equal when no one feels obliged to make an announcement about their sexuality and people just accept each other and who they love regardless of gender" Josie surprised herself with her forward thinking, feeling quite proud of herself.

"Hear, hear," Erin had agreed. "But … you are still going to tell Trev, right?"

Josie had winced. "Yes, love. I'll tell him …soon." Erin was so sweet she had even offered to be there "for moral support" but Josie had declined. "Thank you, but I think I need to do this when it's just me and Trev. Don't worry, I'll keep you posted ... by the way, come round for a cuppa any time you fancy, don't be a stranger."

"I will. I won't " Erin had let out a nervous giggle. She had decided to do her masters degree but was staying at home and commuting. "A lot of the lectures will be on line anyway." She had told Josie who had agreed that there was no point going somewhere further away to pay rent just to sit at a laptop.

And so Josie watched her husband helping her son with his luggage and they had hugged and cried and laughed at themselves and Josie had made sure he had plenty of face masks and fussed about making sure he had hand sanitiser in a small enough bottle that would not be confiscated. Harry assured her for the umpteenth time that he would make contact every day.

"Just so that I can sleep easy in my bed." Josie had explained apologetically. "I'm glad they are four hours ahead there so by the time I go to sleep, I'll know you have survived another day!"

"Flipping heck, mother", Hannah had scoffed. "He's going to work with kids, not enter a bloody war zone."

"So, are you setting me a bed time?" Harry had laughed.

"Just come home safe, my darling boy. I love you so much." She had ignored Hannah rolling her eyes and hugged her son so tightly that he staggered slightly.

"I love you too, mom, thank you for everything."

"I'm so proud of you, son."

Harry looked at her and smiled. "Thank you, mom."

Hannah had gone into the kitchen silently after they had watched until the car was no longer in sight and she had brought them each a glass of wine. Josie had laughed beneath her tears. "Bit early isn't it?"

"What the heck," responded Hannah. "I think you probably need to take the edge off for a bit."

Josie acknowledged that she probably had a point and they sat opposite each other in the living room, which suddenly seemed too big. Soon there would just be her and Trev rattling around the family home, Josie reflected sadly. Hannah's voice interrupted her thoughts.

"So..." her voice was unusually tentative, gentle. "I am guessing that Harry has finally come out?"

Josie was startled. Harry had told her that he hadn't discussed it with his sister. "How did you know?"

"Mom, don't be such an idiot." The scathing tone was back. "Everyone knew …. Well apart from Harry apparently." She laughed. "It's no big deal. Loads of people are gay. Whoopy doo. He just needs to start being honest with himself."

"It's not easy, Hannah. He's such a sensitive boy."

Hannah rolled her eyes. "Can you just do me a favour and wait until I've left for uni before you break it to dad. I really can't be doing with the drama."

Josie shook her head. Very empathetic. She was starting to wish they were both gay. Were lesbians as caring as gay men? She chided herself for her stereotypical thoughts and was glad that she hadn't quite reached that stage of dementia where she voiced her thoughts out loud. God that would be a disaster!

Chapter Thirteen

The next few weeks seemed to disappear in a blur of planning and shopping for Hannah's departure for uni. She was busy seeing friends and working at the pub and Josie, still working from home, tried to stay upbeat and positive around her daughter. Harry, true to his word, messaged her every day and they had spoken a few times on a Whatsapp call. He was looking relaxed and happy, full of his new role and how different life was over there.

"Have you made any friends?" Josie had asked what she thought was a perfectly normal question.

Hannah had guffawed and interrupted. "He's not a bloody child starting school, mom!" and they had all laughed at her.

"Are you being careful?" Josie had persisted. Her latest night worries centred around him being caught with another man and being thrown into jail.

"Yes, mom," Harry had reassured her, "Everything's cool, relax. How are you?"

Bless him, he always remembered to ask how she was and she trotted out the same lines, describing her mundane existence post-lockdown, but, with the nation still being reminded daily of the increased numbers and some areas in local lockdown, it was hard to live life as they had known it. Trevor had tried to persuade her to go for a meal a few times but Josie was conscious of her vulnerability and brushed off the suggestions, saying people were not responsible and she would rather stay safe in her own home. In reality, she wondered whether the truth was that she dreaded that they would sit in some restaurant, just the two of them and have nothing to say to each other.

They all met up on "zoom" the day before Hannah left for uni and more tearful goodbyes were said. Harry was full of enthusiasm for his sister. "You'll have a great time, sis. But don't forget to do some actual studying, that's the whole point of going, you know, it's not just one big party"

"Erm, it won't be a party at all, in case you're forgetting. Social distancing, remember? It's not going to be like your first year, which you probably don't remember, due to the vast quantities of alcohol that you consumed!"

Josie remembered how much she had worried that first year of Harry's uni course and recalled how she used to say how glad she was that he had Erin with him to keep him on the straight and narrow. Haha! That was funny now, she reflected! So, now, secretly, Josie was glad that there would be no house parties for Hannah for the foreseeable future, although she kept reading with a niggle of dread about the illegal raves and parties that the police were having to break up. Hannah was too sensible for that . . . wasn't she . . .?

Josie was delighted to learn that Harry would be coming back for half term in October during the same week that Hannah was due to have a reading week and so had said that she too would be home for a few days. It warmed her heart to know that they would all be together again as a family soon, building some more memories that they could look back on after she had gone. She resolved to be upbeat and positive. She could not leave them with the lasting impression of a miserable old cow, she just couldn't. But it was hard.

Chapter Fourteen

Josie and Trevor had both accompanied their daughter, with Trevor driving the hour and a half to Hannah's uni halls. Parents/visitors were not allowed in and so Hannah had to make several trips to and from the car to her room before all of her belongings had been taken from the car. She could hardly contain her excitement and Josie forced an air of cheerful positivity as she took her last bags and hugged them goodbye.

"Promise you will message me every day" Josie had implored her, just as she had Harry a few weeks earlier.

"Promise, mom, stop worrying."

"You know your mom," Trevor had interjected, "not happy unless she's worrying about something."

Josie had glared at him but held her tongue. What did he know about her worries? Sometimes, he infuriated her.

They were silent on the way home. Josie found it hard to relax in the car regardless of who was driving. Years ago she used to love being in the car, watching the world go by, revelling in the fact that she could put her feet up and sing along to her favourite tunes but as the years went by and she was defined by her motherhood, she became more and more terrified and convinced that they would crash. She was terrified that her children would be left without a mother, or father, or both and once Harry and Hannah started to drive she worried herself sick that they would drive too fast, or text or whatever and that one day she would be that parent who opened the door to a grim faced police officer.

It was not late when they reached home but Josie felt exhausted. She informed Trevor that she was going to bed. She hated herself for the hurt expression that crossed his face.

"I thought we could have a drink." He suggested hopefully. "Contemplate our new life without the kids under our feet." She knew that he was only joking but she had snapped at him and stomped off up the stairs, pretending to be asleep when he joined her a while later. Hours later, when sleep wouldn't come, she logged into her Facebook account and soothed her soul by looking at the messages that Jeff had sent her, reminding her how much he still desired her. Her heart leapt at his invitation to finally spend the night together, the night that she had denied him all those years ago. She wondered now where it might have led, if she had gone through with it. What if Hannah had not caught chicken pox and she had spent the night with Jeff? How would it have changed her life? Their lives? How would it change her life now if she finally succumbed to her desires?

She had fallen asleep in the early hours and when she awoke Trevor was already up. The distinct aroma of a cooked breakfast filled her nostrils. Her stomach did a little somersault of revolt. The thought of eating made her feel sick. The task that lay ahead of her filled her with a sense of despair. She didn't have the energy to deal with the fallout of the news that she was about to deliver to her husband. She pulled on her dressing gown and ventured downstairs. Trevor was singing along to a nineties tune on the radio and smiled at her warmly as if they didn't have a care in the world. Josie sat at the kitchen table and he poured her a fresh coffee.

"Voila Madame." He said breezily. "Petit dejeuner bientot! Breakfast is ready!" He liked to think he remembered his schoolboy French competently but in truth he forgot important things like verbs and subjects and if he couldn't think of the right word; he just used whichever word came to mind. Josie smiled faintly and offered him a small smile of appreciation. He was trying so hard to look after her. She just wished she could stop feeling so irritated by him. "Bientot means soon, Trevor." She couldn't help but correct him.

He gave what he believed to be a French like shrug as he served her a full English. "Pas de probleme, mon petit pois" He grinned widely but as Josie watched him tuck heartily into his bacon and eggs she pushed the food around her plate, conscious of the tight knot in her stomach.

"I have something to tell you." She began.

Trevor looked at her, baffled. They didn't do grand announcements; what was going on?

"What?" He looked at her in mock horror. "You've gone vegan?"

"It's about Harry."

He had been quick to respond at the sound of their son's name. "Harry, what's happened to him? What's wrong?" His face was filled with alarm and he placed his coffee cup down clumsily.

Josie sighed. "Nothing, Trevor, nothing's *wrong*. Everything is perfectly fine and normal. Yes, everything is fine and normal. It's just that he is, well.. he's gay." She heard herself let out a silly and unfamiliar little laugh.

Trevor spluttered on the coffee that he hadn't yet swallowed and stared at his wife. Had she gone completely mad? Harry? Gay? Impossible. He laughed.

"Oh dear, Josie, who's told you that nonsense? " He looked momentarily relieved. Phew, was that it? What a relief. He loaded another forkful of bacon. He was a bit concerned about Josie. She had been acting very oddly lately. He wasn't sure whether it was "The Change" or the Covid crisis, or maybe a combination of both but she certainly didn't seem herself and this was ridiculous.

"Who's been spreading that idea? Haha! Hilarious. Harry is, well, he's in love with Erin, any fool could see that ..."

"Trevor, listen to me." Josie tried to force herself to be patient but she knew that she sounded terse.

"It's not nonsense. He has told me himself. He does love Erin but not in that way. He is not, not, well, not into girls. She's like a sister to him. He likes boys, men I mean." She rushed on, conscious that the colour was draining from Trevor's face as he put his fork back on his plate and shoved his food away, swallowing hard.

Josie continued, desperate for this to be ok. She just wanted to get it over with and carry on as normal. This didn't have to be a big deal. "He has felt that way for a while apparently but it's hard, I suppose, for someone to come to terms with it. I don't know ... I mean ... I haven't been through it myself but it must be hard. Especially for someone like Harry. He's so gentle and not really somebody who wants to attract attention."

Trevor was shaking his head. This was absurd. His son? Gay? No way! Not that he had anything against gays of course, he reassured himself. He pictured Erin as he had expected her to be in the future, the perfect, lovely wife for his son, the doting but sensible mother to his grandchildren. Grandchildren. "What about grandchildren?"

He hadn't realised that he had spoken aloud.

"Trevor," Josie forced herself to sound patient, "It's not impossible these days, he will have all sorts of options, there's adoption, surrogacy ..."

"Adoption! Bloody surrogacy!" Trevor rarely raised his voice but he was clearly rattled at what he clearly found a preposterous notion. "So ... he just uses some random womb to produce my grandchildren? I don't think so! Over my dead body!"

"It's nothing to do with you!" Josie had now raised her voice to match his, "Nothing to do with either of us! Who knows what will happen? And who knows what might have happened if he'd been, if he'd been nor . . . heterosexual . . . We can't plan their lives out for them. They're bloody adults." Josie felt the colour flooding to her cheeks and inwardly chastised herself for the involuntary prejudice that had almost slipped out.

"So, you're telling me you don't care?" Trevor challenged, his voice returning to a more civilised volume but, nonetheless, his tone remained confrontational.

"What do you mean care?" Josie too lowered her voice but the question came out wearily.

"I mean, don't you care that he's bloody gay? Queer? Bent, whatever you want to call it! Whatever you call it, it's not bloody well normal."

"What's normal?" Josie snapped. "And yes, I do care! I am bothered that he's gay, but not in the way that *you* mean."

Trevor looked at her, at a loss to know what she meant. At that moment, Josie felt her irritation turn to contempt. How could he be so blinkered, so shallow, so oblivious to what their son must have gone through, must still be going through? No wonder Harry had wanted to put such a distance between them. He must have known how his father would react. She felt a surge of shame and a rush of love for her son. She began to cry.

"I am bothered," she spoke quietly now, through her tears. "I am worried sick that he will end up the victim of some "gay bashing", that he will be ostracised, discriminated against; I am out of my mind that he has chosen such a gay unfriendly place to hide from us! I am devastated that my son, our son, has gone through this on his own without feeling that he could confide in us. Can you imagine what it must have been like for him? Coming to terms with his sexuality? Knowing that he had no choice but to let Erin down? And worst of all, knowing that YOU would think he had let us down." She spat the last accusation at him as the tears continued to stream down her face.

Trevor, who had always been quick to cuddle her and try to make her feel better whenever she was upset about something, looked at her, looked almost through her. "We can get him help . . . therapy . . . we can sort this."

Josie pushed her chair from behind her with such force that it fell over.

"I absolutely cannot believe you just said that. You disgust me."

That night, Josie slept in the spare room, something that neither of them had ever done before. There had been occasions when one of them had stomped off to begin the night in the guest room but one of them had always given in and they had always kissed and made up. It seemed now that the gulf that had erupted between them was enormous and each of them was locked in their own misery.

Chapter Fifteen

The days that followed their disagreement were some of the most difficult days within Josie and Trevor's marriage. Josie threw herself into her work. She was now going into the office three days a week and working from home for the other two, so it was with relief that she left home each morning and put on her professional face for the outside world. She felt that she had no one to confide in; her argument with Maria had been weeks ago but she had heard nothing from her and Josie had felt too self righteous to be the one to extend the olive branch. She thought about confiding in Jeff but it didn't quite fit with the easy going, frivolous persona that she was aiming to present in their on-line chats.

After three days of avoiding each other, Josie had googled "support for parents of gay children." She had found a support agency that currently offered remote appointments. She was able to secure an appointment for the following week. Feeling that there was a light at the end of that particular tunnel, Josie felt her heart soften slightly towards Trevor. The atmosphere between them had been palpable and it was making her feel completely stressed. She owed it to Harry to try to sort things and get his dad to see sense. She had not told Harry that she had shared his secret with his father and Harry was so wrapped up in his new job that he had not mentioned it. It broke Josie's heart to think that he would find out that his father had rejected him and so she determined to change her husband's stance. She had read similar stories on line and many had a positive outcome following counselling. Trevor had to see that it was he who had to change, not his son!

Trev's latest project was creating a decking area in their garden and Josie greeted him as he came in by handing him a cup of tea. He took it and looked at her sadly.

"I've bought some steak." Josie ventured. "I thought we could eat together."

Trev hesitated slightly. "Ok, thank you, that would be great." It felt ridiculously wrong to be so polite to each other but they had barely spoken in three days.

Josie decided it would be best to wait until they had eaten. Neither of them had eaten properly since the disastrous "petit dejeuner" and so she thought it prudent to at least get some food inside them before attempting to convince Trevor to get on board with the counselling. She had opened a bottle of red, Trevor's favourite, and so they were both beginning to unwind as they finished their meal.

"Thank you, that was delicious." He didn't use her name or call her "love" as he would have done ordinarily but Josie was grateful that the ice had been broken.

"How are you feeling about things?" Josie ventured tentatively.

A look of weariness crossed Trevor's face and she noted that he looked suddenly older. He cast his eyes downwards; not a good sign, thought Josie.

"I can't get my head round it." Trevor shook his head sadly. "Can't believe it. Cannot accept it."

Josie leaned towards him and took his hand as she spoke softly. "There are organisations, people that can help you, us,"

"Help us?" Trevor snatched his hand away. "It's not us that needs the help, is it?" he snapped.

Josie ignored him. "I've made an appointment for us. It's next Thursday at 5 o'clock."

"I'm not going anywhere." Trevor's voice rose indignantly.

"You don't have to go anywhere," Josie tried to keep her voice even. "It's on line. We can do it from here. Together."

Trevor got up and began to clear the table. Josie felt her temper starting to rise. "What's wrong with you?" she shouted. "This is about our son! He needs our support. We have to stand together on this. For God's sake, stop ignoring me!"

Trevor continued to ignore her and began to scrape food into the bin before opening the dishwasher.

Josie had never felt so angry with Trevor and some how she felt vindicated when, later that evening, back in the guest room, she sought solace in her on line chat with Jeff. She knew she was being childish, behaving like a schoolgirl, believing his flattery and giggling to herself as she responded flirtatiously to his messages. By the time she ended their chat, she had agreed to the night away that he told her he felt as though he had been waiting for all his life. She could hardly sleep for the excitement and anticipation that left her physically trembling. It would serve bloody Trevor right, she told herself savagely, he didn't deserve her and he didn't deserve their lovely son.

Josie had it all planned out in her head. She congratulated herself on not having told Trevor about her falling out with Maria. Maria would be the perfect alibi; she would tell Trevor that she needed a break from everything that was going on. A spa break with Maria would be just what she needed as far as Trevor was concerned. Not that he probably cared right now what she did, Josie reflected bitterly. Fifteen years ago, Josie had had to tell Maria that she needed her for an alibi but the ever increasing digital age meant that there was no way that Maria would ever ring the house phone and drop her in it. Deception in the digital age, Josie realised, was so much easier. You could be anywhere you said you were when you answered your phone. As long as she didn't accidentally press video call, she reminded herself, with a horrified giggle, remembering the time during lockdown when she had been on the loo and accidentally answered a facetime call from her boss. Oops!!

Chapter Sixteen

Josie didn't care that she was allowing the gulf between her and her husband to widen. What did it matter anyway, the months were ticking by and she knew that after she had gone, he would probably move on, find someone else. She considered that she should probably seek legal advice regarding their joint financial status. She worried that Trevor would cut Harry off financially after her death and told herself that after her night with Jeff, that would be top of her to do list.

Jeff had sorted the reservation, a lovely country hotel some forty miles away.

"What if we see someone we know?" Josie had worried but Jeff had dispelled this immediately.

"Don't be daft, when did you last bump into someone you know on a weekend break? It just doesn't happen does it? You don't end up in the same hotel as people you know by chance!"

"Actually, there was this once in Majorca ..." Josie had begun but Jeff had cut her off.

"Pah! Majorca maybe. Every man and his dog goes to Majorca – bet it was August?" He nodded smugly when Josie had agreed. "There you are, but we are talking a little hotel a few miles from home." He winked conspiratorially, "The only people you might know there my darling, will be doing exactly the same as us!"

And so the long awaited night of passion was all set for the Friday after the counselling session.

The week or so following the argument passed quickly, with Trevor and Josie pretty much avoiding each other. This was not how she had imagined their lives to be after their children had left home, Josie contemplated with a twinge of sadness, but apart from her obsession with her night away, her number one priority was to get her husband to accept their son's homosexuality. Her stomach was in knots as she drove home early from work on the Thursday afternoon and she found Trevor in the garden, his jeans stained with the dark red colour that he was applying to the newly laid decking. She had reminded him the previous day about their appointment and told him that she would be going ahead with it even if he refused to.

"What are you afraid of?" Josie had asked in what she hoped was an even tone.

"What do you mean, afraid of?" Trevor had turned to look at her and Josie was pleased that at least she had his attention and he was speaking to her. "I'm not afraid. I just don't see the point."

"The point," Josie had returned, "is for us to be able to support our son in the way that he needs and deserves to be supported."

As she approached him now, she prayed silently that he would at least join her in the meeting, listen to what the counsellor had to say. He turned to look at her and she was unable to read his expression. Neither of them spoke for what seemed a life time. Please, say you will do it, Josie willed silently.

Eventually he let out a heavy sigh. "I'll do it." He muttered. "But if I don't like it, I won't stay. I will not be preached at and told I'm wrong."

"It's not about being right or wrong." Josie's voice was soft as she felt relief flooding through her. "Thank you, Trev. Come on, get cleaned up and I'll make us a cuppa."

A short while later, they were forced to sit closer than they had been for weeks as they set up the on line meeting on the dining room table. The counsellor came into view and introduced herself as Ruby. Josie judged her to be in her mid thirties; she was petite, blonde, pretty. She didn't look like your stereotypical lesbian, Josie thought and immediately felt guilty for being judgemental but was relieved that at least she was more likely to make a positive first impression on her now clearly prejudiced and small minded husband.

Ruby explained that they could have as many sessions as they felt they needed. She said that their first session, which was due to last an hour, would be mainly a "Getting to know you" session. She explained that she had helped many parents to come to terms with their son or daughter's sexuality although sometimes, she admitted, she wasn't always successful. She asked them to talk about their family, the lifestyle they had led when the children were younger and Josie painted a picture that she recognised sounded as near perfect as life could be. They had clever and kind children, notwithstanding teenage tantrums, from Hannah in particular. They had had no big medical dramas, no disappointing exam results, lots of happy holidays, often going abroad in the summer and at least one UK break each year.

Ruby had turned to Trevor who had allowed Josie to do all the talking and was sitting awkwardly at his wife's side. "Is this how you would describe things too, Trevor?"

Josie watched as she saw her husband blush slightly and wondered what was going through his mind.

"Yes, that's pretty much how it was." Trevor had nodded in agreement.

"So," continued Ruby. "How did you feel when Harry came out?"

Josie sensed Trevor stiffening beside her and he took a long breath. The silence that followed made Josie nervous but she forced herself not to speak for him.

"It's ok." Ruby had spoken eventually, reassuringly. "Trevor, many many parents, in fact most, probably, find it difficult at first to accept that their son or daughter is gay. For many, it's like a grieving process. Parents feel grief for the person that they believed their child to be. It's probably harder if the child reaches adulthood before they come out and I gather from what you've said, Josie ..." Ruby consulted the information sheet that Josie had submitted previously. "I gather that Harry had a long-term girlfriend, is that right, Trevor?" She spoke to him directly and Trevor nodded, his lips set grimly.

"That's not unusual either," Ruby continued. "And you mustn't feel duped. It was not an intentional cover up. If we can try to think of how confusing it must have been for Harry, how frightening, trying to fit in and also not to let you down. Do you feel let down, Trevor?"

Trevor shuffled uneasily in his seat and nodded again.

"That's ok." Again Ruby spoke reassuringly. "We can work through that."

"Work through it!" Trevor spat the words contemptuously. "The only thing I want to work through is what we can do to . . . to cure him!"

"Ok," Ruby was calm and Josie realised that she had had these conversations many times. Just how many priggish parents were out there she wondered. "You say cure him. That's interesting, Trevor. Do you think Harry wants to be cured?" She paused but Josie could tell that she didn't expect Trevor to answer. "You see, what you are suggesting is effectively "gay conversion" and whilst it is not yet illegal, it is likely to become so in the not too distant future. It's another step that needs to be taken in the equality fight."

Trevor stood up abruptly. "I've had enough of this bollocks." He left the room and Josie faced Ruby, embarrassed.

"It's ok," Ruby spoke quickly and firmly. "Don't worry, Josie, I've seen worse."

Josie felt the tears threatening and she held back a sob. "I don't know what to do. It's like I don't know this man at all. This is not the man I was married to and ... and ..." The tears now were streaming down her face, "And Harry . . . my son is not the son I thought he was . . . I'm such a failure and . . . and I'm ... I'm dying."

Ruby now was shaken. "I'm so so sorry, Josie . .. what ... I mean ... do you want to talk about that?"

Josie shook her head and wiped her hands across her face, clearing away the tears. "No," she sniffed, "I'm sorry . . . I didn't mean for that to come out. I don't want to talk about it. It's ok. I'm ok with that . .. "

"But ..."

"No, really, it's ok. I just want to get everything sorted for Harry . . . before ... before I . .." Her voice tailed off before she hastily added "Please don't mention this, I haven't told anyone else."

"Ok, I understand. You have so much on your plate, Josie, and everyone has already been through so much this crazy year. Listen, I think we've done really well in getting Trevor to at least attend the meeting. It's a huge step, honestly. Some people never even get that far. It's so sad." The sound of genuine sadness in Ruby's voice clutched Josie's heart and she found herself wondering about this apparently self-assured young woman; what was her story? Did she speak from experience? Josie realised that she had presumed she was gay but of course she didn't need to be gay to be doing this job and yet she sounded so briefly forlorn, Josie wondered if this beautiful young person had been abandoned by her own parent or who even knew what her story was.

Ruby quickly gathered herself and continued. "Look, I'll send you some links. See if you can get Trevor to have a look at other parents' stories. There are some really moving cases - all true - where parents have struggled with anger, disappointment and there have been estrangements that have gone on for years sometimes but there are some really reassuring happy endings, I promise you."

They had booked in for the same time the following week and Josie had closed the laptop, unsure of whether she should feel optimistic or despair. She felt exhausted with emotion and uncharacteristically, a short while later, fell into a deep sleep on the sofa.

Chapter Seventeen

Josie awoke blearily , a patch of dribble sticking her mouth to the cushion. She heard the sound of the front door closing and shortly afterwards, the slam of a car door. Trevor, she processed, was leaving for his early shift. He must have seen her asleep, still in last night's clothes, but had chosen not to wake her and she tussled with her emotions; was she relieved that she would not have to face him before leaving for her date with Jeff or was she hurt that he was choosing to widen the ever-growing chasm between them? She rose unsteadily and headed into the kitchen, where she put the kettle on and glanced around her. The vacant stools, the tidy counter, everything felt so empty. She sighed and yawned. Conscious that she must look an absolute sight, she walked into the hallway to face herself in the mirror. Over recent weeks she had read how the lockdown and the subsequent widespread working from home had led to an upsurge in women seeking cosmetic surgery and other alleged rejuvenating products after weeks of looking at themselves reflected back from their zoom screen had left them feeling insecure about their appearance. Josie had felt a sense of relief in realising that it had not just been her who had looked at herself in horror, especially when nowadays all her colleagues seemed to be younger, flawless and confident. She ran her fingers around her face; had she really started to look like her mother? She lifted her breasts to where she thought they would have been and sighed. Who was she kidding? Why would Jeff find her attractive? She snorted derisorily, men could always find a younger woman if they wanted, why was life so unfair? Wrinkles and grey hair on a man were apparently distinguished but on a woman they just labelled her as "past it" and women just gradually became invisible.

"For god's sake, Josie, stop feeling sorry for yourself!" Josie chastised herself sharply and forced herself to dig deep for some inner strength and motivation. "Right, today, is all about *you*, Josie Winters! You've done a fantastic job bringing up two wonderful children. You've kept yourself in ok shape. (compared to some, she thought, thinking of some of the sights at the gym!) Your bloody, stupid husband doesn't deserve you. So *you* are going to have some *fun!*"

Josie had bought some new pampering products and treated herself to a leisurely shower, scrubbing the exfoliating polish into her skin and revelling in the feel of the hair mask, that for once she had time to leave on for a full fifteen minutes. She was careful to pack everything in her overnight bag that she would need for a spa break, not that Trevor would check, she knew, but she realised with a thrill that the sense of deception was actually awakening feelings that she had thought were long dead. She was starting to feel really turned on at the thought of her night away with Jeff. She fingered the silkiness of the new underwear that she had smuggled to the back of her wardrobe as she now packed it carefully along with the new, short, silky kimono. She had planned ahead! She wasn't sure that she had the confidence to walk around a hotel room in her underwear!

She deliberated about whether she should text Trevor but then reminded herself that he was not supposed to have his phone on at work. Perfect, she would just scribble him a note. "Booked the day off. Going for spa day/night with Maria. Lasagne in the fridge. See you tomorrow." Her pen hovered – kisses? Her heart hardened. No, no kisses for Trevor. Not now.

Josie and Jeff had agreed that they would drive separately to the hotel. Josie drove with the music turned up, listening to 90s classics, firing herself up for the afternoon and night ahead. She arrived, deliberately fifteen minutes late – she had no intention of walking into the hotel bar, where they had arranged to meet, by herself and she knew that she would be too nervous to stand side by side with Jeff checking into a double room. "I am such a prude." She giggled to herself, thinking about that now as she drove along the hotel's sweeping driveway.

She walked into the hotel lobby and saw that the bar went off to the right. Jeff was sitting so that he was visible from the lobby and she spotted him straight away. He was dressed immaculately, in a pale blue shirt and expensive jeans. His shoes were casual but well-made and shiny. He strode toward her confidently and kissed her on both cheeks, his smile wide, his teeth, she noted, were very white.

"Josie, darling, it's so good to see you."

She smiled, opening her eyes wide, hoping that her wrinkles were as attractive as his. "You too, Jeff." Her voice came out breathlessly and she willed herself not to be nervous. She wanted him to believe that she was every bit as self-assured and confident as he was and as the persona she had tried to portray on line. Today she was not the anxious mother, the disappointed wife, the rejected friend (who was also dying, reminded that nagging voice.) Today, she was Josie, successful accountant, independent woman, exciting lover …

"What can I get you to drink?" Jeff was guiding her into a seat opposite where he had been sitting.

Josie didn't hesitate "What gins do they have?"

"What? Who the hell said that?" Josie's inner voice was yelling! She never drank anything other than pinot or prosecco, well, apart from champagne at weddings and special birthdays. Young people drank gin, who was she trying to kid?

He winked, clearly impressed that she was intending on a relaxing afternoon. Josie looked around nervously whilst he caught the eye of the bar maid. It was table service only in these unprecedented times. She breathed an inward sigh of relief. The hotel was practically dead and there was definitely nobody there she knew.

Josie was surprised how easy it was to relax in Jeff's company (maybe the two gin fizzes helped a lot) and an hour later, she was feeling giggly and adventurous. The bar overlooked the hotel's swimming pool and she realised that it had been a genius idea to pack her swimwear.

"Did you bring your trunks?"

Jeff was confused and looked at her questioningly.

"Let's go swimming!"

"But …"

"Come on, it'll be fun!" Josie giggled and looked around. "Back in a sec." She walked with what she hoped was confidence, glad that she had forced herself to eat some breakfast that morning, conscious that her head was slightly fuzzy from the gin that she was not accustomed to.

The young girl on reception gave no indication that she thought that Josie was tipsy, so Josie took that as a positive and after speaking with her for a few moments, returned beaming to Jeff, who was watching her with interest.

"They sell swimwear! Come on, let's go!"

Minutes later they stood side by side in the lift, each of them standing next to their cabin cases, their free hands touched fleetingly and as their eyes met, they both smiled.

"I've waited a long time for this, Josie." Jeff turned and leaned towards her as she closed her eyes waiting for the kiss that she had feared would never happen. A split second later, they sprang apart as the lift bleeped noisily, announcing their arrival on the second floor.

Their room was a uniform four star double, nothing particularly individual or quirky but for Josie the room was unique in its promises of thrill and seduction. Josie was nervous and eager that they should not just jump straight into bed together. She wanted some sense of freedom, exhilaration and the lure of being in their swimwear together, not quite naked and not able to touch in public, gave the afternoon a sense of suspense and adventure.

"Are you sure about this?" Jeff ventured, "Swimming I mean?"

Josie grinned. "Well, I'm not that bothered about swimming, but the water looks lovely and it's been ages since I've been in a jacuzzi or a sauna."

He grabbed her hand and pulled her towards him. He cupped her face in his hands and smoothed back her hair. "Oh Josie, you look beautiful when you smile. I've missed you."

Josie looked up at his face, he looked so sincere. She didn't speak but placed her own hand on his face and soon their lips were touching. The strangeness of lips other than Trev's on her own sent a strange sensation coursing through her body but she knew that it was not one that she was going to reject. Her body was filled with anticipation, stepping into the unknown, no going back. Their kiss was slightly awkward at first as their mouths adjusted to the newness of the other. Josie wondered fleetingly if it was the same for him, had he been faithful to his wife all this time, she mused. She dispelled the thought instantly. What did it matter? She had made up her mind, she wanted some fun and she was going to have it.

Jeff's hand began to wander down her body and Josie felt the stirrings of desire but then she remembered the pool and the fun they would have. Keeping him wanting would be part of the pleasure. She pulled away, breathless. "A lovely hors d'oeuvre, Jeff," she giggled, "But let's not rush to the banquet!"

Jeff looked at her longingly and she revelled in having the upper hand. She held all the cards and she would keep him guessing and wanting. "Come on, grab your stuff, we need to go and buy you some swimwear, unless you want to get us thrown out of here!"

A short while later, Josie looked nervously at her appearance in the full length changing room mirror. There had been another lady, probably a bit younger, getting changed at the same time and Josie had taken a sidelong glance at the other woman's cellulite, smugly revelling in the fact that she had kept herself in pretty good shape for her age. She was aware that in certain lights she had a few very faint feathery lines on her tummy but she prided herself that she had worked hard to maintain her slender figure. Tonight she would be with someone who would actually appreciate it, she thought rebelliously, thinking momentarily that she couldn't remember the last time that Trevor had truly looked at her. She glanced at her face and decided that the best thing she could wear to complement her wrinkles and to defy the slight sag of her chin would be a dazzling smile. She practised now in front of the mirror before looking around foolishly to check she was alone. Not allowing herself to hesitate, she stepped boldly towards the exit of the changing rooms and towards the pool. Shoulders back, Josie, she told herself, tummy in, think tall. She spotted Jeff lounging in the corner of the pool, his lower body submersed beneath the invitingly clear water. She noted the greying hairs on his chest but his body was in pretty good shape and she plastered a dazzling smile on her face as she walked to the edge of the pool. She lowered herself gently into the pleasantly warm water and swam over to him.

"Wow, Josie, you look amazing." He grabbed her hand and pulled her towards him. Her wet skin was touching his and she realised that she was no longer faking her smile.

"Thank you, Jeff." she was delighted by the attention. "You don't look too bad yourself. How are the swim shorts?"

"A bit tight." He groaned meaningfully and Josie shook the water from the ends of her hair as she giggled at his innuendo.

"Race you to the other end." she challenged and, freeing herself from him, she set off towards the end of the pool, which was in fact probably only about ten metres away. They were both breathless however as they reached the end of the curved pool, which was not exactly designed for training. She remembered that they had been drinking alcohol and she realised that she was breaking all her own rules, normally so careful and safety conscious, she was glad that her children were blissfully ignorant of her recklessness.

"This was a great idea, Josie." Jeff looked at her, admiringly. "I'm glad you are not one of those women who's scared to get her hair wet. Josie pulled her hair away and up from her neck and squeezed the water. "It won't take long to dry." It sounded like a promise. She was conscious that they would not be wanting to waste any time.

Somehow they managed to while away an hour and a half in the pool, the jacuzzi and the sauna. There were a few other people around and so for the most part they managed to keep their hands to themselves but they sat closely and allowed their fingers to entwine and their thighs to touch, which sent a tingling sensation through Josie's body as she felt her nipples screaming to be touched beneath her wet swimsuit. They chatted idly about places they had been and places they wanted to see. The lockdown experience had put paid to most people's holidays but the travel companies were putting their all into trying to lure back the bookings. Josie's stomach had clenched into the now familiar knot of fear, knowing that her own future was limited and that she would now probably never see the Grand Canyon or take the river cruise down the Danube that she always said they would have once the kids were older. She forced the thoughts out of her head. There was nothing she could do about what was to come. For now, she had to live for the moment. Her body was still telling her that she was young and full of energy and that was the reality that she chose for today.

They were in the jacuzzi for the second time when Josie looked up suddenly and saw that the pool clock was showing almost five. They had a dinner reservation in the hotel for seven and she looked with horror at her fingers, which were now taking on a prune-like appearance.

"After you" Jeff said gallantly, nodding towards the steps. Josie smiled as she realised he would be studying her behind as she climbed out of the pool.

Chapter Eighteen

Maria was busy preparing the evening meal, half listening to the radio when yet another report came on, warning that the second wave of Covid 19 was now imminent. The prime minister had announced that restrictions were once again being increased and from the following week it would be illegal to meet more than six people. Tighter restrictions were in place for a number of towns and cities around the country and Maria's heart sank as once again the news that this virus was not going away any time soon hit home. She worried daily about Mark's condition and in spite of his outwardly healthy appearance, she lived in fear of his health worsening and his vulnerability rendered her livid at the people she saw in the media recklessly failing to social distance, going about their lives with careless and callous complacency. She and Mark had not been out much at all and the lack of company was beginning to take its toll on Maria, who was normally such a sociable person. They went out for their daily walk and some days they ventured further, travelling by car to canals, rivers, forests and other countryside locations where, mostly, they felt comfortable enough to walk around mask-free. The weather continued to be unpredictable, with no two days seemingly alike. Maria tried to stay positive and she was looking forward to her new life as a grandparent. She was becoming alarmingly addicted to online shopping and already had a considerable stash of baby clothes and other essentials in preparation for the birth and beyond. As she chopped at vegetables with a force that belied her inner frustrations, she realised not for the first time how much she missed her friend. With a sigh, she put down the knife and picked up her glass of chilled white wine. She had seen little of her own children, both of whom now had flats of their own with their respective partners and so, with the restrictions that had been in place, they had had to rely on text messages and WhatsApp calls, all a far cry from the usual, weekly family get-togethers that she had cherished.

"What's up, love?" Mark had walked into the kitchen and was quick to pick up on her mood.

She turned and walked towards him, losing herself in a bear hug, holding him tight as if her life depended on it. She didn't realise that she was crying until she tasted the salty tears on her lips.

"Hey, come on, what's the matter?" Mark's voice was full of concern.

"Everything!" Maria exclaimed, choking back a sob. "Everything's a mess! I can't stand it. The whole year has been a write off and it's just not getting any better. I just want ... I just want everything to be back to how it was ... and I'm terrified of anything happening to you!"

"Nothing's going to happen to me." Mark held her away from him and wiped away her tears gently, kissing her salty mouth and cupping her face in his hands. "We have to stay positive. I'm lucky - I get checked every six months so if anything is going on, they'll know about it."

"But it's the word …"

"I know." Mark knew what she meant. The C word, Cancer, the L word, Leukaemia, they sounded horrific, terrifying; he could not relate the words to his body that still did everything he expected it to do. He still looked the same when he looked in the mirror and when he looked down at his hands, they were the same; when he awoke in the mornings, he felt no different but it messed with his head sometimes, the thought that there was this potentially deadly disease lurking in his blood. He found himself feeling guilty if he allowed himself to feel self-pity. There were so many people dealing with so much worse but sometimes he wished he had a cancer that could be cut out, burned off, got rid of and thrown away, not a cancer that resided like some squalid squatter, waiting to make its move. Or not. He had to cling to the fact that many people, as the consultant had assured him, lived long and healthy lives and died of something completely unrelated to the condition, hopefully merely old age. This was the stance that he maintained in front of Maria. He couldn't let her see that he too worried about it daily, constantly alerted to the slightest twinge, looking for signs that were not there and then worrying that worry would be the thing to trigger a worsening of the condition.

"But look," he said brightly, "I'm absolutely fine. I'm not going anywhere. You . . ." He kissed her emphatically. "You are absolutely stuck with me." He smiled down at her and pushed her hair away from her face, where it had become stuck to the wetness left by her tears. "Why don't you let me finish preparing dinner and you go and have a nice bath. Take your wine. Tell google to play something relaxing!" He placed her wine glass in her hand and directed her out of the kitchen. "Go on, off you go." He patted her backside and she turned to him with a smile. "Don't be so daft," she scolded herself, "He's absolutely fine."

A short while later, she sank into the bubbles and breathed a relaxed sigh as the wine started to help her unwind. Her thoughts wandered to Josie and she thought sadly of how much she missed being able to share her worries with her life-long friend. She wondered if she had taken heed of her words or whether she had proceeded with her plans to pursue her liaison. Had she been too harsh? Maybe she should have encouraged her to talk through why she was feeling tempted by an affair rather than just jump down her throat. Perhaps Josie was right, maybe she had actually been hypocritical ... god, what a mess everything seemed to be at the moment. Maria scooped the bubbles and stroked them against her skin, lost again in thought. She sat up and drained the last of the wine from her glass. "Right," she resolved. "Enough is enough. Life is far too bloody short." Who knew how short ... Tomorrow she would go and see Josie. She would apologise and she would listen and she would support her and she wouldn't be such a bossy, self-righteous bitch. And she would tell her the truth about Mark and hope that her friend would forgive her when she realised that she had been living under a cloud of worry and pressure even bigger than the Covid nightmare that was blighting all of their lives.

Chapter Nineteen

Maria walked towards Josie's familiar front door. She smelled the flowers that she was carrying as a peace offering and breathing in the sweet scent helped to quell her nerves. She had slept well after a relaxing evening snuggled up with Mark, finishing the bottle of wine as well as another. Later they had made sleepy love and he had held her tight, telling her how much he loved her. She had counted her blessings. Whatever the future held and, right now, the only sure thing was that it was uncertain for everyone, she thanked her lucky stars that fate had brought Mark into her life and brought her the stability, the love and quiet adoration that she had missed out on for so long. Today, she would put things right with Josie and that part of her life at least would re-gain its equilibrium.

She had to ring the doorbell twice before she heard movement. There was a car she didn't recognise on the drive and she remembered that Trev's car had been stolen so assumed he had a new one and that Josie's was in the garage. Briefly she had wondered whether they had gone out for a walk; the day's weather looked promising , with a clear blue sky and a warm breeze. She was starting to feel deflated, disappointed and so she was relieved and delighted when finally the door opened slowly. She was nervous but smiled in anticipation of putting things right with her friend.

"Trev! Hi!" Maria faltered as she took in Trev's dishevelled appearance, unshaven, with bags under his eyes, his clothes hanging loosely, giving the impression that he had lost weight. "God, Trev, are you ok?"

He ignored her question and she realised that he was staring at her with a look of complete alarm on his face. "What are you doing here? Where's Josie?" His voice rose to a panic. "Has something happened? Is she ok?"

Maria stared back and tried to make sense of what he was saying. Was he drunk? What was he talking about …?

"Erm." Maria's mind was racing. What was going on? Where was Josie? How long had she been gone? "Trevor," Maria looked around her. Whatever was going on, she was guessing that this conversation was not one for the neighbours. "Can I come in?" she faltered.

Maria placed the flowers on the kitchen counter, noting the coffee cups and plates stacked in the sink and several empty beer bottles lined up by the bin. It was clear that something was very wrong. Josie normally kept the kitchen in pristine order.

Trevor had closed the door and followed her the short distance into the kitchen. She turned and faced him. "What's going on?"

She couldn't read the expression on his face. "You tell me …" He looked at the flowers and his mind was working overtime. Maria was here to see Josie, she wasn't bringing him flowers was she … "She's not been with you, has she?" He spoke slowly and she sensed his defeat.

"I … I don't know what's going on Trev … I'm sorry." She started to babble. "Me and Josie had a fall out … I've lost track of time …weeks ago … didn't she tell you?"

Trevor shook his head miserably, colour creeping up his neck as he processed his wife's betrayal. "She told me she was on a spa break … overnight last night … with you."

To Maria's horror, she realised that Trevor was going to cry. His face crumpled and he placed his head in his hands. She rushed to his side, hesitating fleetingly as she remembered social distancing and her husband's vulnerable status. Goddamn, bloody virus, how could you stop yourself touching people you cared about when they were distraught? She rubbed his arm, feeling inadequate. "Let's sit down. I'll make us a cuppa. I think you could do with someone to talk to."

"Is she having an affair, Maria?" He looked at her and she knew how hard it was for him to ask, desperate to know the truth and desperate for it not to be true.

Maria sighed. "I don't know, Trev, honestly, I don't." It was the truth, she told herself, she didn't actually know what Josie was up to. "We haven't spoken in weeks."

"But why would she lie?" The anguish in his voice tore at her heart. "She told me she was on a spa break, with you."

"I know, Trev. You said. I don't know why she would lie." She felt herself clutching for straws. Maybe there was another explanation, one that didn't involve bloody Jeff whatshisface.

"Have you two been getting on lately?" Maria enquired, her mind working overtime. "I'm sorry, I don't mean to pry, I'm just trying to figure it all out."

Trevor wiped his eyes with the heels of his hands.

"No." He said quietly, "We're barely speaking. Everything's gone to shit."

Maria was shocked but at the same time relieved that maybe there was another explanation. "So, maybe she's just gone away to sort her head out. It's been such an intense time for everyone. Covid bloody 19, gloom and doom on the news and flashing up news alerts on your phone every five fucking minutes. She probably just needs to escape for a bit." She perked up as she started to believe her own version of events. "She probably just didn't want to hurt your feelings by saying she wanted to be on her own."

Trevor shook his head. "Has she told you about Harry?"

Maria looked up sharply. "No, what about Harry?"

Silence filled the room and then slowly, Trevor pulled out a stool and sat with his head in his hands. He began to howl. Maria was filled with total panic. What on earth had happened to Harry? Her heart was racing. She pulled out the adjacent stool and shook his arm almost violently. "Jesus, Trev, what the hell has happened to Harry? Is he ok?" The previous weeks of not speaking to Josie flashed in front of Maria and she felt a deathly panic take hold of her heart. What on earth had been going on whilst she had been sulking with her friend …

She shook his arm again, "For god's sake, Trev, please tell me what's going on."

Trevor was sobbing now. She had never seen a grown man in such a state. She placed her hand over her mouth, filled with an intense fear of whatever it was… The moments hung suspended in the air and finally when she thought that she could bear it no longer, he blurted out "He's gay."

Relief flooded so fast through Maria's veins she heard herself let out an involuntary laugh. She caught herself quickly, this was not as straightforward as it should be. Clearly Trevor was devastated.

"Oh Trevor…" She rubbed his arm now, desperate to console him, to make everything ok. "Trev," she murmured softly, "I could have probably told you that years ago."

He looked up, his eyes bloodshot from crying, his face perplexed. "What? Really?"

Maria smiled softly. "Does it really matter? He is still the same boy … man." Maria realised that she wasn't remotely surprised to find out that Harry was gay but she frowned as she contemplated the fact that it had never come up in conversation between her and her best friend. Had Josie known and how did she feel about it? She was baffled.

"I can't … I can't handle it." Trevor was shaking his head. "I'm not . . . I'm not homophobic …. I'm not." His voice was persistent and she wondered who he was trying to convince. "I even voted for that Will Young, you know, years ago. Well it was so obvious wasn't it?" He half laughed, half sobbed. "It's just different when it's your own flesh and blood."

"Look, Trevor, go and wash your face … and brush your teeth!" I am going to put the kettle on.

Maria needed to think. She packed him off and filled the kettle, her friend's kitchen as familiar to her as her own. Where the bloody hell was Josie, she thought with a flash of anger. But she didn't know who she was most angry with. She should not have shut Josie out, she chastised herself; she should have sensed that there was more going on in her friend's life than just her fragging' libido. She thought about her own worries over the past months and how she had kept them to herself. At a time when they had needed each other more than ever, how had they managed to end up so far apart? She quickly wiped away a tear as she heard Trevor heading back down the stairs.

"That's better." Maria smiled with a brightness that she hoped hid her underlying sense of being completely out of her depth, terrified of saying the wrong thing, making things worse. She placed two mugs of steaming tea in front of them. "Have you eaten lately?" He looked as though he hadn't had a good square meal in quite some time.

He shook his head. "I'm not hungry."

"Ok," she conceded. "So, let's talk." She referenced back to his earlier comment. "When you say that it's different with your own flesh and blood, what do you mean?"

He sniffed and shook his head wretchedly but he had regained some composure and she sensed that he wanted to share his burden. "I don't know." He rubbed his forehead heavily as if trying to work out some great mystery. "I just feel .... "

"Come on, Trev, it's ok, just say what you feel, get it out."

He managed a sardonic smile. "We've been to a counsellor."

"Okay ... " Maria was momentarily confused. Was he talking about their marriage now?

"To try to help me understand." Trevor clarified.

"I see ... and has it helped?"

He half laughed but she feared he might start to cry again at any time. "Does it look like it?"

Maria positioned her lips into a grim smile. "Sorry, stupid question."

There was a pause, the tension was beginning to ease as she felt again that he wanted to get it all off his chest. She reached over and held his hand, shrugging off the momentary tensing in her stomach reminding her of social distancing rules and her husband's condition. "I won't breathe a word, Trevor, honestly".

"I just can't get my head around it." He confessed quietly. "I mean what about Erin? He's had a bloody girlfriend practically since he could walk."

She let him talk.

"I feel ... as though he's died . . ." A tear fell from his eye and he wiped it impatiently with the back of his hand. "He's not who I thought he was. Everything's changed. I mean ... you know, I just imagined him and Erin, nice little house, a couple of kids. I thought we'd all go on holiday together and me and Josie would help out, do everything right, you know."

Josie started to speak but he interrupted. "Please don't mention surrogacy or adoption. I can't cope with it. Am I being selfish, wanting my own flesh and blood ... *normally ...?*" He paused. "Am I allowed to say that word?"

She ignored the last question. "You're not being selfish, Trevor, it's just come as a shock and it will take some time to get used to but let's face it, did you do everything the way your parents wanted? You can't map their lives out for them!"

"That's what Josie said." He admitted. He looked up at her, shamefaced.

"And this isn't a choice." Maria added. "It was how he was made. It's not some perverse phase or immoral lifestyle. Lots of gay and lesbian couples stay together for a long time ...get married ..." She glanced at his face, "Okay, sorry, I'm going too fast."

He shook his head. "I know, you're right. I know. It's just hard."

The sound of a key in the front door broke the silence that followed and they looked at each other in alarm. Maria willed the ground to open up so that she could just disappear. She couldn't be part of whatever was about to take place.

She stood up. "You know where I am if you need me, Trev, stay calm." She patted his arm and gave him a meaningful stare as Josie entered her kitchen and witnessed her former best friend and husband looking very, very cosy.

"What the hell …" Josie stared at the scene in front of her. "What the hell is going on with you two."

Maria opened and closed her mouth. Trevor leapt from his stool, "Are you for fucking real?" His tone was filled with disbelief and disgust.

Maria interjected. "Look, you both need to calm down." She couldn't read the expression on Josie's face. She looked genuinely shocked to see the two of them sat in the kitchen, it was almost as if she hadn't used Maria as an alibi at all … She looked from one to the other and picked up her keys, glancing briefly at the flowers that she had brought as a peace offering. Not really the time, she told herself. "I'm going to go." Neither of them looked at her, they were staring at each other, anger and hurt filling both of their faces. "Try not to kill each other." She muttered as she made a hasty retreat to the front door, where she let herself out. She breathed out heavily as she stood for a moment on the front step. They wouldn't would they? She thought in a moment's alarm … surely they wouldn't actually kill each other …. Oh my god, you heard about these things on the news … this could not be happening.

"Morning dear!" Maria was brought to her senses by the shrill tone of Josie's nosey neighbour. "Everything ok?"

"Splendid, Cynthia!" trilled Maria with mock cheerfulness. "The country's in total chaos, the Brexit deal looks shot to pieces, half the country is heading back to lockdown, the NHS is threatening strike over their lack of pay rise when they have just shed blood for the county. Everything is just bloody spiffing, wouldn't you say?"

Cynthia's mouth dropped open.

"Have a lovely day, your geraniums are looking positively blooming." Maria hastened to her car and almost in one movement, was moving away from the kerb. Her hands were shaking on the wheel and she had to pull over once she was out of sight of the house. She actually thought that she would be sick. How much worse could things get?

Chapter Twenty

The previous evening.

Josie was glad that she had packed to pamper, her skin was definitely feeling the effects of the extended exposure to chlorine. On returning to the room, they had kissed and once again Josie was filled with desire and fought the urge to give in there and then.

"You're not teasing me ... again?" Are you? Jeff had held her tight and momentarily she had felt a sense of panic, his tone was slightly accusing.

"Don't be silly," Josie had kissed him long and hard and her spine had tingled as their tongues entwined. "I just want it to be perfect .... not rushed."

"There's no saying we can't do it more than once, you know." He whispered provocatively in her ear. "I'm no lightweight."

Josie had giggled but wriggled herself free. "I stink of chlorine ... and I'm starving. I need some food to soak up that gin but I promise you, feed me and I'll be all yours."

She had hummed to herself in the shower, feeling freer than she had felt for ages. She did not allow herself to think of home, of Trevor, of Harry or Hannah. This was about her for a change. She bloody deserved this. She had dressed carefully in the new underwear that she had bought on the internet. Since lockdown they had had so many deliveries, Trev didn't bat an eyelid nowadays when a courier van turned up. It was the new normal. She had been delighted with the fit when she had secretly tried on her silky new purchases and over the days running up to their triste, she had found her mind drifting to the prospect of Jeff running his fingers over her skin, gently peeling off the garments ... And now the night had arrived, she was consumed by her lust for excitement and passion, she needed so much to feel desired and to desire.

The effects of the gin had worn off by the time Josie held Jeff's hand and walked with him into the hotel restaurant. Momentarily, she had almost lost her nerve at the prospect of being seen but Jeff had squeezed her hand and winked at her confidently. They had chatted easily over their two courses, which were served at a leisurely pace and somehow, Josie had realised that they were a considerable way down their second bottle of wine as she felt her inhibitions slipping away. It was shockingly easy to avoid talk of spouses and offspring. Chatting about their holiday dreams, Josie had quashed the feeling of panic and sadness that threatened to destroy her relaxed state as she contemplated that she would be highly unlikely to fulfil her dreams. Her inner voice had interrupted her thoughts and had reminded her that that was why it was all the more important to live for the moment.

In spite of starting to feel the effects of the red wine, (red had been Jeff's choice - it was years since she had drunk red wine and she suspected that it was somewhat stronger than her usual eleven and a half percent pinot grigio), she had gone along with Jeff's suggestion that they have a liqueur and the Tia Maria had slipped down easily, leaving her feeling warm and confident. As she took her last slip, she felt Jeff's hand on her thigh under the table and as their eyes met, they both knew that they would not be able to hold out any longer. Their passionate kiss in the lift this time went undisturbed and Josie was thrilled at the thought of what lay ahead.

As they stood in front of their hotel room, their arms wrapped around each other and Josie giggling like a schoolgirl, Jeff swore as they both realised that his key card was not functioning. "Shit" he muttered impatiently, "I'm bloody dying for a pee."

"I'll go down to reception, " Josie offered brightly. "Shouldn't take long."

Famous last words. The queue probably looked longer due to social distancing, Josie realised, but it would appear that there were quite a few other guests having similar issues. It was only as she stood there that she realised that she had not thought to try her key, which she now fished from her bag ready to hand over. Finally, after drawing upon all of her reserves of patience and smiling with false gratitude at the girl on reception, she was making her way back toward their room.

"Oh!" Josie exclaimed out loud, realising that Jeff was no longer waiting in the corridor. Josie was mystified. How had he got in? Had the key worked after all after she had gone down to reception? She placed the new key card tentatively over the lock and it obligingly lit up green. She put the smile back on her face in readiness to be swept into Jeff's arms and on to the king-size bed that Jeff had been careful to request. She closed the door quietly and turned the corner to face the bed.

"Jeff?" she called out questioningly.

Jeff was spread-eagled diagonally across the bed, his mouth lay open as his head lolled to one side and Josie became aware of the deep snores which resonated around the room.

"What the ..." Josie was staggered. He had clearly not been awaiting her return with quite the excitement that she had expected. "Jeff!" She called his name loudly. Nothing. "Jeff!" She was aware now that her voice had become quite shrill. Not at all the sexy tone of a would-be mistress. She walked to the side of the bed and leaned over to shake him.

"What the fuck!" Josie was suddenly filled with total outrage as she looked at Jeff, snoring and ... was that dribble on his chin?! Did she really want to wake this man, this virtual stranger, this ...

somebody else's middle aged husband to … to fuck her?

Josie retreated hastily to the en-suite bathroom. Oh my god. She was shaking inside. What the hell am I doing? she asked herself silently. She gazed at herself in the mirror that filled the entire side of the bathroom and she recoiled in disgust. The chlorine and the alcohol had done her no favours. Josie began to cry and still shaking she started to sweep up her toiletries into the washbag that she had abandoned earlier. Back in the bedroom, Jeff's snores seemed even louder and he had rolled over on to his side, his hand curled protectively and pathetically on his crotch. Josie threw her things into her suitcase – they had not exactly unpacked – and moments later she was calling the lift. She had not thought about the prospect of sharing the lift and shrank in horror as the doors opened upon a young couple whose laughter stopped suddenly when they took in Josie's dishevelled and distraught appearance.

"Are you ok?" the young girl spoke softly and Josie nodded, unable to make eye contact.

The girl cleared her throat. "There's a lot of upset around at the moment with this bloody virus. Are you sure we can't help you with anything?"

Attempting to muster some sense of dignity, Josie nodded again and muttered something along the lines of having just received some bad news. Well, it was not exactly an untruth she reminded herself.

It was pretty bad news that Jeff had apparently waited so long for this moment and had then clearly found her so unappealing that he had fallen fast a-fucking-sleep. Fresh tears spilled over and she felt them sliding down her neck. "Sorry," she muttered somewhat unnecessarily. She knew that as soon as she was out of sight, they would forget about her and go back to enjoying whatever joke they had been sharing before her untimely intrusion.

Josie was back at reception, which was now thankfully, much quieter. She pulled herself together and put on her best business voice. "I am so sorry, I have just had some bad news and need to leave. Please could I check out early?"

"Of course, Madam, I'll just bring up your details." Josie watched as her brightly coloured nail extensions danced daintily across the keyboard. "Has everything been ok with your stay?"

Was she serious? Josie nodded politely. "Er actually, could I just pay my half of the bill? My . . . er ... friend will settle his half in the morning."

The young girl looked unsure for a moment and studied Josie's face as if trying to decide if she looked like a con artist.

"That will be fine." She smiled vacantly and in the silence that ensued, Josie found herself studying the unlined face, the painted eyebrows, the lack of dark circles. She felt like a hag.

"Have a safe journey." the receptionist smiled brightly as Josie placed her credit card awkwardly back in her purse.

Josie practically ran to her car. Thank god they had arrived separately. She was driving along the winding drive towards the gateway and on to the main road before Josie was suddenly jolted by two realisations.

One. She couldn't go home tonight.

Two. She was about to drink drive.

Fuck.

Josie pulled up before the gateway and ran around to the boot of her car where she always kept a supply of bottled water. Just in case.

She downed most of the half a litre of water in almost one gulp and groped around in her bag for chewing gum as if that was going to help sober her up. She couldn't believe that she was going to do this but her satnav was telling her that there was a Premier Inn a third of a mile away. A third of a mile. She could do this. Couldn't she?

Ok, she instructed herself as she pulled out of the gate, be careful. But not too careful, don't want to attract attention. Oh my god, what if she killed someone? Or herself. She realised that the latter option was not the worst one right now but she thought despairingly of Harry and Hannah. Was this the last memory that she wanted them to have of her? She drove nervously and after a few minutes along the straight road, she rounded an island, aware that she was taking it too widely. Breath, stay calm, she reminded herself .

Josie had thanked god (the one she didn't believe in) as she saw the sign for the Premier Inn just yards away.

What if they had no vacancies? Josie realised that she would have to sleep in the car, which was now parked precariously just centimetres from the tree that she had somehow failed to notice as she had come to a sudden standstill, completely forgetting to change down her gears.

Chapter Twenty One

Josie had checked in and found herself in a sparsely furnished but clean single room. She had lain on the bed, curled up into the foetal position and broke her heart. She felt so lonely, so full of despair; confusion and self-loathing mingled with feeling like a complete idiot. She literally felt as though she wanted to disappear.

She had been awake until the early hours, eventually falling asleep with exhaustion but her mind was filled with worries about Harry in Dubai and Hannah at uni and the fact that she had almost thrown her marriage away. She didn't know which parts were dreams and which parts were her waking thoughts but she awoke feeling as wretched as she had when she had fallen asleep. Her mouth was as dry as feathers and the face that looked accusingly and disgustedly back at her in the bathroom mirror was haggard with sleep deprivation, mascara-streaked tear stains tattooed across her cheeks. All that pampering gone to waste she thought miserably. She looked ten years older. At least. How on earth was she going to convince her husband that she had been on a spa break? He would tell her to get a refund. It was only when she had awoken to see three missed calls and a text message from Jeff that it occurred to her that he must have slept for hours without even realising that she had gone. The first missed call was at 5.10 a.m. So much for his eager anticipation and the fact that he had apparently been waiting for that night for years. What a silly old fool she was. So, she was a prick teaser?! I think the term is "LOL" she had muttered to herself as she blocked his number and deleted him from her contacts.

She had showered , cursing herself for not bringing more bottled water from the car and so had drunk about two pints of hotel bathroom tap water, which made her gag but she felt so dehydrated, inside and out. She could still smell the chlorine on her skin. At least that would serve as some evidence of the "spa break", she thought bitterly. By the time she was driving down her road, she had started to convince herself that she looked reasonably normal, having applied a fair lashing of concealer and blusher to bring some life back into her face. Her emotions were in turmoil. She didn't know if she felt more angry with Jeff or with herself for their disastrous romance. When all was said and done and in spite of all his sweet nothings, he was just somebody else's boring bloke. How could she have contemplated having sex with him? What the hell was wrong with her? She had felt an overwhelming and belated sense of loyalty to her husband. He had been with her through everything, always, and she felt sure that he would never, ever cheat on her. He was just too ... too... she didn't know what it was ... unimaginative ... unadventurous ....maybe, she accepted, but there was one thing for sure ... he was too bloody honest. Never in her wildest dreams could she imagine him chatting someone up, conducting a secret affair or even giving in to a moment's temptation with anyone else. All of the effort that she had been putting into livening up her own love life, she realised sadly, should have been put into rejuvenating her life with the man to whom she had avowed loyalty and fidelity.

She wondered later how she had failed to notice Maria's car which must have been parked not far from their driveway. She never had been one for noticing whose car was whose and so she had breezed into the kitchen, preparing to put her all into repairing things with Trevor. She would forgive him his difficulty in accepting Harry's homosexuality. They would deal with it together and they would be there for their son, together. At least, for as long as she had left on this earth.

* * *

Josie and Trev stood staring at each other across the kitchen. Josie heard the door close behind Maria and turned momentarily, trying to assess the situation. She took in the flowers on the counter and slowly the truth seeped awkwardly into her tired brain. Maria had come to see her, not Trevor, she had come to try to recover their lifelong friendship and now that chance too had been destroyed. She looked back at Trevor. The hurt that was etched into the lines on his face was a look that she knew that she would never, ever forget. What oh what had she done ...?

"Trevor …" She went to step toward him, raising her arms to reach out to him.

"Don't fucking touch me!"

Josie recoiled. Trevor had never sworn at her in all their years together. She shrank from his look of disgust.

Josie felt the heat rise in her neck and suddenly she was boiling hot, she felt as though she couldn't breath. Was this her first hot flush or had she got the bloody coronavirus …"Trev, please …. I feel …. I don't feel …"

"YOU feel?" Trevor exploded. "What about how I fucking feel? Where the hell have you been?" He glared at her, outraged. "No," he held his hand up, "Don't fucking tell me. You absolute bitch. I don't want to know."

Josie watched as he shook his head and then walked slowly to open the cupboard where they kept their keys. He took his car keys.

"Please, Trevor." Josie rose from her seat and was sobbing now. "Please let me explain. I need to tell you … everything."

He looked back at her one last time before turning towards the hallway and the front door. "I don't want to know." He muttered coldly.

Josie heard the door slam and she slumped back down, her head in her hands, sobbing.

Chapter Twenty Two

Trevor was gone for most of the day. Josie spent the day accompanied only by a sense of numbness. She had stared at her overnight bag, standing untouched on the kitchen floor. The disgust that she felt with herself threatened to consume her. She tore off her clothes where she stood on the kitchen floor and bundled them into a bin bag, as if she were handling clothes from a murder scene. She took her second shower of the morning and washed her hair furiously, desperate to rid herself of every last scrap of the contamination that she felt from her time with Jeff.

"But we didn't do anything!" She spoke the words out loud to herself as if to try to convince herself of her innocence. "Please, god, I don't deserve this, please make everything ok."

She had no desire to do her hair or put on any make up and she dressed in joggers and an oversized tee-shirt before pulling on her trainers and throwing the overnight case into the boot of her car, swiftly followed by the bin bag. Ignoring Cynthia, who she vaguely heard calling out to her, she slammed her door shut and headed for the local tip. She flung the case as far as she could into the skip, ignoring the bemused stare of the orange clad worker who she guessed would be in there minutes later, checking for anything of value (or maybe evidence of a crime . ..) Again, she felt a rush of hotness creep up her neck and she scurried red faced to her car.

She had no idea how she would get through the day or the weekend. She had sent perfunctory messages to Harry and Hannah and they had dutifully replied. She hoped that their reassurances that everything was fine were a bit more genuine than her own. If ever they knew what was going on at home, she would die of shame. Maybe she actually would, she pondered. Maybe she would go even sooner than she thought. Consumed with self -pity, Josie cried on and off for hours but made some use of the day by logging on to her laptop and deleting all trace of Jeff. She logged into work as the only way that she could think of to distract herself from her misery. Intermittently, she picked up her phone and checked for messages. None from Jeff, because he was blocked. And none from Trevor because ... because he despised her ...

In desperation, she tried to call Maria but she was clearly not interested in speaking to her either. Josie remembered the flowers that Maria had brought round and she was filled with shame. She wondered if she could ever win back her friend's respect after this. Maria had clearly been prepared to extend the olive branch and try to resurrect their friendship. Had she really thrown away not just her marriage but her closest friendship too? She couldn't bear to look at the flowers that she didn't deserve and Josie found herself coatless and cold, walking towards the cemetery that was a ten minutes' walk from home. She wandered around as if in a trance, staring at the tombstones, some of them had been there decades but others were much newer and with a shock she took in just how many people did not reach old age. She was going to be one of those people. She didn't want a tombstone, she realised, she just wanted to disappear, to be forgotten. She couldn't face the thought of the mess that she had made of her final year. Overwhelmed with self-pity, she lay the flowers on the grave of a woman unknown to her who had apparently been a beloved wife and mother and yet the vase that stood in front of her name was empty.

She walked home beneath a sorrowful drizzle; she realised that her fingers were numb and her eyes were streaming from a combination of tears and the wind.

Trevor was back, she realised with a stab of what felt like terror. She had no idea what to expect. His last words to her rang in her ears. She recalled his coldness, his swearing, the look in his eyes. Only a miracle could bring back the safe, steady, predictable husband that she now yearned for but knew that she had treated with contempt. His disgust for her was no less than she deserved and nothing compared with the disgust that she felt for herself.

"But nothing happened." Again the voice in her head, her sense of self-preservation kicked in and she realised that her only chance of saving her marriage was to convince Trevor that it was her choice not to go through with the infidelity. She shuddered with repulsion, recalling the sight of Jeff, snoring and dribbling when she had been hot with lust, believing herself irresistible to him.

Trev was sat in the kitchen, nursing a cup of coffee. She tried to read his body language, the look on his face, but he gave nothing away. She went to sit beside him, suddenly conscious that she must look an absolute sight. Her hair was frizzy and unkempt and she thought of how the cold would be emphasising her wrinkles. She lowered her head but looked up sharply as he spat the word "Don't" and put his hand in front of the stool to block her attempt to sit by him.

"We're done." He said flatly and she shook her head not understanding, or not wanting to understand.

"Done?" she repeated dully, "What do you mean?"

"Divorce. I am going to divorce you. You can move out as soon as you like. I will keep the house for the kids to come back to and when they are settled, we can sell and you can go to hell with your half as far as I'm concerned."

"Trev, love . . . come on ..." Josie made a half laugh, half whimpering sound. "You don't mean that. You're upset. Let's talk this through ..."

"There is absolutely nothing to discuss." He enunciated every word carefully, a steely expression on his face. Again, she tried to reach out to him and again he rejected her. He looked her fully in the face. "I have devoted my entire adult life to you and our family, Josie. I have never, ever, ever ..." his voice trembled slightly but he checked himself before he continued, "never betrayed you, never even been tempted."

Josie tried to interrupt him, the voice in her head screaming "But nothing happened!" But he was intent on having his say and his voice rose with a mixture of anger and indignation, "Don't you think there have been times when I've felt bloody bored, wanted a bit of attention? Because that's what it boils down to isn't? You wanted some bloody attention, some bloody middle-aged crisis. Do you not think we've enough crises going on without your antics? Did you even think about Hannah and Harry? Even if you didn't think of me? How do you think they are going to feel, when they find out that you're ... an ... adulterer?"

He spat out the word as if she were a whore, or a murderer and she shrank from the coldness in his voice. She didn't have the energy to argue. "But nothing happened." The words didn't come out, they simply resounded in her head. Mentally destroyed, she fell to her knees, buried her head and wept.

She sensed Trevor standing up and his words tumbled around her ears. "You're a pathetic mess."

Chapter Twenty Three

October arrived, cold and wet. The news was still full of the Covid crisis. The virus was rearing its head again with local lockdown restrictions in place in various UK locations. There was a 10pm curfew on pubs, restaurants and clubs and the rule of six meant that social gatherings were heavily restricted. The American president and his wife were the latest high profile figures to test positive and a Scottish M.P. had broken the law by travelling four hundred miles by train after testing positive. It seemed as though the world had been turned on its head and it was taking Josie an inordinate amount of willpower to get out of bed in the mornings after one sleepless night followed another. She thanked god that she had work to keep her busy and for at least part of her day she was distracted from the disaster that had become her life. Trevor had taken to preparing his own meals, washing his own clothes and they had barely spoken in the days that followed his announcement that he wanted a divorce. They had been due to meet remotely with the counsellor but Trevor had told her that he was not going to be participating. Josie had seen no point in going ahead by herself and so had cancelled the appointment. They had not mentioned their children and she wondered if Hannah and Harry thought it odd that their parents had taken to texting them individually.

Somehow they had sat together and maintained a front when Harry had skyped them. He was so full of his own news that he had seemed not to notice their minimal contributions to the conversation. There was little that most people had to say anyway these days, people were existing in a vacuum of going to work (with many still working from home or furloughed), the supermarket and little else. Josie knew of a few people who had been abroad but most people had shunned the idea of wearing a mask throughout the whole airport and flight experience and the ever-changing quarantine rules meant that if you were brave enough to go, you might find at any point that you would be required to quarantine on your return. There seemed no escape and no end in sight until a successful vaccine could be found and universally implemented. Harry reported that unlike the UK, Dubai had been successful in instituting some of the strictest lockdown measures in the world and consequently appeared to have the virus under control. Nevertheless, as in the UK, schools could again be forced to resume remote learning if there were to be a confirmed case within a school or a "bubble". Josie worried that he was on his own a lot when not working but Harry assured her that he had made friends and was well and happy.

It was during the Skype call that Josie had first realised that she had developed a cough. Trevor had noticed too and as soon as the call ended, he sprang away from her.

"You need to get a test"

"What?" She knew what he meant but she found herself asking stupidly, "A covid test?"

"Yes, of course a bloody Covid test." He threw her a look of disgust. "Though god knows whether you need any other type of test." He left the room and she heard him upstairs, opening and closing wardrobe doors and drawers. She went upstairs and saw with rising panic that he was packing a suitcase.

"You need to self-isolate." He offered in explanation. "It's easier if I go."

There was nothing she could say to argue with his logic but the thought of being alone in the house for potentially two weeks filled her with alarm. The burglary had left her feeling edgy whenever she was on her own especially.

"Where will you go?"

"I'll find somewhere." She noted sadly that he had not asked her how she felt or shown any regard for the fact that she might actually have the deadly virus. Josie realised that she really did not feel too good. She had been feeling so wretched lately that she hadn't noticed that she actually felt awful. Her throat ached, she felt so weak and she realised that she felt inexplicably hot, not to mention the damn cough that left her feeling breathless. She googled how and where to get a covid test and managed to get an appointment in town for the following afternoon. She took herself off to bed for the remainder of the day and feeling utterly exhausted, she had fallen into a fitful sleep, disturbed by bouts of coughing.

The following day, dosed up with paracetamol, she dragged herself off to the pop up test centre. The test was unpleasant, involving a swab of her nose and throat and she returned home feeling worse than she had ever felt, both mentally and physically. Again, she took to her bed and tried to rest. She was afraid and she missed Trevor so badly. She missed her children. She missed her life.

Harry and Hannah were much more concerned than her husband she noted with relief but she reassured them that it was just a precaution. Much as she wanted to be cared about, she didn't want to cause them to worry. She knew that they loved her and that they would be devastated to lose her; she was sadder for them than she was for herself, she realised.

"I'm worried about dad," Harry had confided suddenly "He doesn't seem himself lately. Have … have you told him?"

"What?" Josie had been so wrapped up in herself she momentarily wondered what he meant. "Oh, sorry, Harry, yes, yes I did."

"And?"

Josie hesitated. She could not tell her son the terrible truth. He would feel so rejected. "He is ok, ish ... it's a lot for him to take in, " she attempted a laugh which she knew sounded fake, "you know your dad, he had it all planned, you and Erin, a nice little semi and a couple of grandkids."

Harry had looked at her curiously, as much as you could look at anyone properly via Skype but he didn't probe any further. Instead he broke the news that he was no longer allowed home at half term due to travel restrictions. Josie automatically felt a sense of disappointment but then swiftly realised that it was for the best. He would be so upset to discover the dreadful state of his parents' marriage, not to mention his father's inability to accept his homosexuality. A couple of days later, unsurprisingly to Josie, Hannah also announced that her reading week was cancelled and she would not be home either, probably until at least Christmas. Josie thought about the prospect of Christmas with horror.

It was two days before she got her Covid test result. She spent much of the time trying to sleep and she tried to force herself to eat. With no sense of smell or taste and a heightened state of anxiety, food was the last thing on her mind but she so badly wanted not to have the virus and to be better. She was not surprised when she received the text message confirming that she was positive. At least the pain in her body masked the pain in her heart. She knew that she needed to let Trevor know. They had sat next to one another, used the same kitchen if not the same bathroom, so he too could have caught it. Summoning her courage, she rang his number and heard it ring twice before he clearly rejected her call. Not wanting to leave a voicemail, she resorted to texting and kept it brief:

"I have tested positive. You will need to isolate and get a test. Hope you are ok?" She typed in her standard three kisses before deleting them and pressing send.

She could see that he had read her message instantly but it was several minutes before he sent a brief reply, which simply stated "OK"

To Josie the lack of apparent care or compassion was like a body blow but a few moments later, Trevor was ringing her. She had been mid cough and it took her a few moments to reply, swiping frustratedly at the phone, desperate not to miss the call.

"Hello" Her voice was barely audible.

"Christ." Trevor sounded shocked. "Are you ok?"

Tears pricked behind her eyes as she recognised that he did still care … maybe … "I'm ok . .. feels like the worst dose of flu you can imagine."

"Is your breathing ok?" He spoke hastily as though in a panic.

"Yeah, I'm ok. Do you feel ok?"

"I'm fine. Just bloody irritating having to self isolate if there's nothing wrong with me."

"I'm sorry."

"It's not your fault." For a moment his voice was soft but then he coughed awkwardly and briefly as though he had recalled the stigma attached to coughing.

"Can we ..." she wanted to ask if they could talk but she was stopped mid sentence by another bout of coughing. She had to hang up and he texted her a few seconds later.

"Let me know if you need anything."

"Thank you. Xxx" She typed the kisses and pressed send before she could allow herself to change her mind. Her heart felt lighter for having had something resembling a normal conversation with her husband. She had to win him back, for as long as she had left. Maybe she should tell him that she was dying . . . or would that be emotional blackmail? Her thoughts were racing but she felt a warm, glimmer of hope that the small time that she had left could be positive and that her husband and children would have happy memories of her and them all as a united family.

The days that followed were hard. She felt so ill that she barely left her bed. By some miracle, or act of fate, Trevor's test came back negative. Josie told herself that it was karma, she deserved it and he didn't, simple. She also convinced herself that he was only staying away from her because she had to self isolate and that once she was better, everything would be back to normal.

Chapter Twenty Four

For Maria the "second wave" of Covid was even
more disturbing than the first. She would not have
believed that it could have been possible but now
that numbers of those infected and dying around
the globe were again rising, the scenario seemed
to be far worse for those considered clinically
vulnerable. The first time around, the lockdown
and subsequent shielding measures had seemed
harsh but necessary in order to save lives and
when Mark was diagnosed, she was relieved that
he would not be going back to work until it was
safe to do so. Now that they were both back at
work and the government had no plans to re-
introduce shielding on the grounds that
workplaces were now considered "Covid safe", the
reality was that as far as Maria was concerned
they were dicing with death every time they went
to work. Maria worked as a senior purchaser for a
local steel company and Mark was a secondary
school teacher of maths. Maria found herself
ranting daily at the politicians on the television,
the government had made one u turn after another
and there was criticism from the opposition party
as well as scientists regarding the government's
failure to control the deadly disease. The latest
confusion came from the three tiered lockdown
rules that put some areas in complete lockdown,
whilst another limited social gatherings to six and
a middle tier prevented households from meeting
up indoors but shops and restaurants remained
open albeit with a 10 p.m. curfew. Maria, along

with millions of others could not understand the logic that said that someone could work in a pub but could not meet their mate in the pub! Teaching unions were battling for a two week "circuit breaker" and so Maria was praying that that would bring some respite at least from the relentless worry. She frequently felt the urge to stand on the top of a mountain and scream; but there was nowhere to run to and nowhere to hide. She could not understand those who continued to gather in large crowds, ignoring the rules and seemingly believing that they were immune or invincible. On the day of the first 10pm curfew there was an apparently impromptu cricket match, with a distinct lack of social distancing, held in a London street. Being turned out of the pubs at ten, for some, simply meant that the party continued in someone's home. Realistically, there were not enough resources to police the rule breakers and anyway how could people be expected to follow the rules when the very MPs who proposed them were themselves breaking?

Maria missed her friend. She felt an almost permanent sense of sadness at the loss of their friendship but she was also still inwardly seething with Josie for what she considered her foolishness and selfishness. She didn't doubt that Josie was probably bored and in need of some attention but did that justify hurting a man as loyal as Trevor and destroying their family unit? She realised that she secretly thought that Josie had had things a tad too easy and now was throwing it all away just as easily. Nevertheless, Josie had been her closest friend and she missed having her to sound off to; she could imagine what Josie was thinking about the mess that the government was making in its handling of the ongoing crisis. She was curious as to how things had gone between Josie and Trevor after she had left them staring at each other in the kitchen; she had felt tempted to contact Trevor but this had seemed like a betrayal and she was not yet ready to forgive Josie, so it was easy to let the rift between them continue. She threw herself into looking forward to the arrival of their first grandchild. At the moment they were still in tier one and could still meet their grown up children who did not live with them. She hoped fervently that the whole Covid nightmare would be over by the birth so that they would not be forced to miss the precious early weeks and would be able to support the young couple as they embarked upon the rocky road of parenthood. There had been stories in the news of first-time moms giving birth without their partners and grandparents separated for months from their beloved grandchildren. None of it was like anything anyone had ever experienced or could have imagined.

As half term approached, it became clear that there was not to be a circuit breaker in time to extend the standard week's holiday and so Maria resigned herself to the fact that her husband had just one week's respite from the strain of being surrounded by teenagers who seemed incapable of comprehending the importance of social distancing. She wondered whether she had ever had that sense of invincibility that made young people drink too much, drive too fast, take a pill from a stranger or in 2020 just stand too close. She went shopping and stocked up on fruit and vegetables, fish and chicken and planned lots of healthy meals for their week off. She wanted more than anything to have a few nights away at the very least in the countryside but could not bring herself to suggest to Mark that they risk his health by staying overnight anywhere other than their sanitised home.

"I can't face being on my own, Mark." She confided in her husband over dinner on a wet and windy mid-half term evening. "I know it's you that has this condition but I am so scared that it's me who will be left on my own and that we won't have the retirement we have worked for, planned and hoped for."

Mark had reached across the table and taken her hand. "None of us knows when our time is up ... I'm lucky now because I get checked," he said pragmatically. "I'm fit, well, ish," he grinned, patting his midriff, "I've hardly ever had a day off work. Please stop worrying. As soon as this is all over, we'll get our lives back on track, we'll have loads of things to look forward to."

Maria had allowed herself to be consoled and as if to prove his point, Mark had made love to her that evening with such passion that she had temporarily allowed herself to believe that nothing had changed and they would still have decades together. It was a different story, however, in the early hours, when she awoke with the familiar stomach full of dread and her mind full of what ifs. She wondered how people coped with losing a partner and felt a physical sense of being completely unable to cope if she were to find herself alone again.

Chapter Twenty Five

Halloween and bonfire night were looming, albeit with bans on trick or treating and organised events. Young people, however, were videoed mocking the police as they partied in the streets and ignored instructions to socially distance and not mix with other households. The government had lost its credibility and rumours of a second lockdown were leaving people worried for their businesses and their jobs. The track and trace system had been ineffective and unreliable and the race to find a vaccine continued amidst disturbing concerns that immunity may last for just a matter of weeks. Wales, along with France and Germany, was in the midst of a second lockdown as the daily number of infections and deaths returned to worryingly high levels with the disease continuing to strike indiscriminately.

Josie was finding it hard to regain her strength, although the worst of the illness appeared to have passed. She was left struggling for breath merely climbing the stairs. She had just got to the top of the stairs on the last Saturday in October when the doorbell rang, causing her to have to retrace her steps, trying to remember if she was expecting any parcels.

"Oh!" Josie's mouth fell open at the sight of her husband whom she had not seen for over two weeks.

"The key's in the door." He offered by way of explanation, "So I couldn't get in."

"Oh." Josie appeared to have lost the ability to process thoughts or words and for a moment simply stood and looked at him. He looked thinner and tired but there was a hint of kindness in his familiar eyes and her heart leaped at the possibility that he was coming back to her and not just the house.

"So, can I come in?" He asked slightly awkwardly, looking around , expecting to catch a glimpse of Cynthia who never seemed to miss the slightest prospect of any gossip.

"Sorry, of course!" Josie stepped aside self-consciously, suddenly aware that she was in her old but comfy dressing gown, her unwashed, unbrushed hair was scraped back into a scruffy ponytail. "I was just going to go and get a shower." she said hurriedly, lest he should think that this was how she had intended to spend her day.

"Don't mind me." He called breezily as he strode off towards the kitchen, dropping his bag in the hallway. "I'm going to get a coffee and then get ready for the qualifier."

Josie turned towards the stairs, hiding her smile. She remembered how irritating she always found the grand prix - the same noise, the same names every week, it all seemed ridiculously boring but impossibly dangerous to her. Now, though, she realised that the thought of her husband back in their home would render the roar of the engines and screech of the tyres music to her ears. She found herself humming to herself in the shower. Was this it, she thought, was he back? They had been in frequent but polite communication whilst she had been isolating and the subject of them divorcing had not been brought up. She ignored the voice in her head that reminded her that, for her, it was irrelevant anyway as her days were numbered. She took her time getting ready. She had not realised that she had lost several pounds and her standard look of jeans and sweater left her looking shapeless. She blow dried her hair carefully and selected a skirt and top that did not accentuate the need for her to regain a few pounds.

He turned to face her as she walked into the living room.

"You look nice." Trevor had never been big on compliments even when she fished for them so from him, this was a major turning point. She opened her mouth to protest, knowing that in spite of her efforts, she looked pale and thin. She checked herself just in time however and instead Josie smiled properly for the first time in many weeks.

"Thank you. Are you hungry?"

"I'm okay at the moment." He pressed pause and the bright red F1 sports car was instantly stopped in its tracks.

"Look, I think we should …"

"Stop!" Josie blurted, putting up her hand to silence him. She didn't know what he was about to say but she was afraid. Without thinking, the words spilled out of her mouth "I'm dying."

He gazed at her, not comprehending, "I don't understand. You said you felt better, that you had finished isolating …"

Josie shook her head and in spite of herself and her freshly applied make up, she began to cry. He left his chair and pulled her to the sofa, where he sat her down carefully as if terrified that she would break.

"I don't understand," he repeated, "Josie, stop it, you're scaring me . . . tell me what's going on."

"I don't know." Her earlier light spirits had given way to a feeling of forlornness and hopelessness and suddenly the pressure of the preceding months, bubbled up like some powerful volcanic eruption and she sobbed relentlessly whilst Trevor rubbed at her arm and her back and desperately tried to make sense of what was happening.

"I'm dying." She repeated, her voice filled with despair. "I'm going to die … soon … within months."

He shook his head, mystified, afraid. "You're not making any sense, Josie … what's wrong with you?

Have you seen a doctor? Is it ... cancer?" The words were falling out of his brain and out of his mouth before he had even processed them as thoughts.

"What?" Josie paused and looked into his terrified eyes.

"A doctor . . . have you seen a doctor .... what have they said?"

"No ... nothing ... it's not like that ... I don't know." Suddenly Josie sat bolt upright and put her face in her hands. After a long pause, Josie whispered "Trevor ... I think I might be losing my mind."

He kissed her hands tenderly, consumed with a rush of emotion and the will to protect her. He kissed away the tears that were spilling through her fingers, down her wrists.

"I'm going to get some tissue and a glass of water and then you are going to tell me everything ... ok?"

She sniffed, embarrassed to see droplets of water falling from her nose. He kissed the top of her head as he stood up. "Good job, you're now covid free with all that snot you're dripping over me."

She gave a half sob, half laugh and wiped at her nose with her hands in what she recognised as a completely covid unfriendly manner. She looked around for sanitiser, which was now a feature in every room.

He came back with a toilet roll and a glass of water, placing the latter on the coffee table in front of her and tearing off a lengthy stretch of tissue.

"Right. Start at the beginning." His voice shook a little. He had no idea what was going on but in the past few days he had realised how much he loved his wife and now, as he took in her words, the prospect of her dying was more than he could bear. With the threat of the virus having finally become real and personal, his anger had subsided and whatever she had done to sully their love, the fact remained that she had been the biggest part of his life for so long. He reached over and took her hands in his. "Josie, speak to me, what's going on?"

As she looked at her husband and felt his hands holding hers, she became overwhelmed again with emotion and the sobs that moments ago she had brought under control returned.

"Josie, you are frightening me. Please tell me what's happened. Are you sick . . .?"

She was trembling and sobbing and could barely speak. "I ... I think .... I need something stronger than water."

"I'll be right back." He walked into the dining room and opened the drinks cabinet that they hardly ever touched. He had no idea what was even in there, just whatever had been left from the previous Christmas probably. He grabbed the first bottle he saw and poured them both a generous measure of brandy. He took a large gulp himself before returning to his wife who was breathless from sobbing.

"Here, drink this."

They sat for a few moments and Josie allowed herself to be soothed by the alcohol. She closed her eyes and exhaled deeply. She placed the glass on the coffee table and took a handful of tissue to clean and dry her face. Her face was red from crying, mascara streaked down her cheeks and Trevor realised that he had never seen anyone look so full of anguish.

"I need to get this straight in my head." She said quietly.

"Ok, take your time."

She recalled the moment vividly when she had learned that she had a year to live. She remembered the confusion, the anger, the fear, the heartbreak that she felt at the prospect of leaving her family, never seeing her children settled, married. She recalled the pain of realising that she would never cuddle her grandchildren or spend leisurely, retired days with her husband. She remembered the terrible sensation of feeling that her life had not been enough, that there was still life to be lived. She recalled with shame the selfish and superficial relationship that she had forged with Jeff and how she had tossed aside Trevor's love and risked everything.

"Oh God, Trevor." She gripped his hands desperately. "Have I lost you?"

Trevor was thrown. He was expecting her to tell him some dreadful illness. She had told him she was dying. He had no idea what was going through her mind.

"I don't know… Josie … I don't know what you mean. I am so confused."

"Will you hold me?" her voice was tiny, vulnerable.

His heart filled with love and at the same time gripped with fear. He pulled her close and held her.

"I'm so sorry." She spoke in his ear whilst he stroked her back and her hair.

"Sh … Josie …. Let's not talk about that now." He had instinctively known that she was talking about her deception and not her illness.

"I need to tell you Trevor. I am so sorry, I lied to you but I was … I was never unfaithful to you. I never have been."

He kissed her hair but pushed her gently away so that he could look into her eyes. "So what happened?" He asked quietly. "I need to know."

Did he? Josie asked herself. Did he really need to know the truth? Would it be ok if she bent the truth, just ever so slightly so that he didn't stop loving her? She knew now that she had been a fool, craving attention, wanting to be desired when in reality she had more than any woman could wish for. Trevor was still not a bad looking bloke and he was utterly, utterly loyal; she trusted him more than she trusted herself. Maria had been right, she realised sorrowfully, she should have been looking to re-light the fire in her own marriage, rekindle the passion with her own husband not conduct some sordid little affair with someone who probably didn't think twice about cheating on his wife. Oh my god, she realised in horror, what if she had caught some horrible infection. She shuddered visibly.

"I promise I didn't sleep with anyone else."

He looked at her and she felt as though the eyes that she had known for so very long were penetrating her soul. She pulled him towards her and kissed him tentatively on the lips. At first she thought that he was going to resist but within seconds he was kissing her back and they lost themselves in each other.

"Come with me." He took her hand and pulled her towards the stairs.

Their love making was tender but desperate and completely intense. Neither of them spoke until they both were lying breathless in a post-coital haze. Josie felt weak, covid had taken so much of her strength.

Trevor pulled her close. There was still something he just didn't understand. His desire for his wife had overwhelmed him and he believed that she had not betrayed him – he had no choice because he knew that he couldn't give her up. But... She had told him she was dying. What happened to that conversation? He rubbed his forehead in confusion.

"Josie..." She didn't respond. He said her name again before realising that she had fallen asleep. He stroked her hair, realising that she was exhausted. She had just fought off a potentially deadly disease. He held her and let her sleep until he felt sure that she would not be disturbed if he let her go. Whatever was going on, she clearly needed her sleep and the grand prix had just started.

Chapter Twenty Six

Josie slept for over two hours. She could still taste the alcohol and her head felt heavy from crying, drinking and sleeping deeply. It took her a few moments to remember the events prior to falling asleep but a smile formed on her lips as she hugged the pillow against her cheek. She felt happier than she had felt for what seemed like an eternity. She recalled how Trevor had held her, said her name, told her he loved her over and over again and she had told him she loved him too. How could she have risked losing everything? She shuddered at her own stupidity. And then she remembered the conversation that they had abandoned. She swung her legs off the bed and went into the en-suite to freshen up. When she came out, Trevor was sat on the bed waiting for her with a cup of tea.

"You ok?" He pulled her towards him as he asked the question.

She nodded, feeling self-conscious. Her eyes were puffy and she looked drained. The virus had taken its toll.

"I feel such an idiot."

"Well, surely, that's nothing new?" He laughed at his own joke as he pushed her hair off her face. "Do you want to try again .... to tell me what's been going on?" He was suddenly serious. "What did you mean by you're …. dying?"

Josie put her hands over her face. "I *am* an idiot." She insisted.

"Ok, well, we can agree on that if you like, but just, please, tell me."

She took a deep breath. "Since my birthday, or thereabouts, I have honestly believed that I had less than a year to live."

"Why would you think that?" Trevor was baffled. She had said that she hadn't seen a doctor …

She shook her head and covered her face with her hands as if in disbelief at her own stupidity now that she realised that she had in fact been a fool in more ways than she had thought.

"I got this message thing … on my phone ….it was during lockdown …. everything had gone a bit crazy, nothing seemed real any more …."

She was gabbling and he stroked her hand. "Take your time."

She gave him a weak smile. "So, I got this message thing from a … you know… a spiritualist type person … medium … or whatever … saying that I could have a free reading."

Trevor was struggling not to laugh out loud. Jesus, did people actually fall for that stuff? "Go on." he said patiently, noting the blush, which was creeping up her neck.

"So, I followed the link and I put some details in about myself and got this personalised reading. Lots of it was true, you know, about the number of children I have and what they would do for a living but then it said that … that I was going to die … in a year."

"And you believed it?" Trevor tried to stop his voice sounding incredulous, aiming for an empathetic tone. Poor Josie, she had actually been torturing herself with this crap!

"I know." She held his gaze and shook her head. "Honestly, Trevor, I think I must have lost my mind or something. I've been in such a state, I really believed I was dying. And I felt … cheated … like, something I was entitled to was being taken from me. I felt as though I had had less than everybody else was going to get so it made me ….I don't know I just felt dissatisfied with everything … and kind of depressed …" Her voice tailed off.

"And then you met someone on line?" He didn't mean for his voice to sound hard and bitter but it brought back the terrible memory of Maria arriving and finding out that his wife had lied to him. It tore him apart to think of her in someone else's arms, someone else touching her intimately, it was more than he could bear. He needed to know the truth. "What happened? Where did you go? How far … how far did you go?"

She knew that he wasn't asking how far from home they had been but he continued before she could speak "Who was he? Christ, Josie. He could have been some bloody rapist ... or ... or murderer?"

She shook her head as if to say she wasn't that stupid but in reality she wasn't sure that she wasn't. To what lengths would she have gone to get some attention?

She spoke quietly and told him that it was someone she had known from work years ago.

"Oh my god, so you have kept in touch all this time?"

"No!" she protested. "No, it was just through stupid facebook, he looked me up, probably looks up loads of people" she said hastily. He didn't need to know about her dalliance fifteen years previously. Her marriage was salvageable so she definitely needed to hold back on some of the facts. She told him the name of the hotel that they had been to.

"We just had lunch and then swam in the pool for a bit and then later ... at dinner ... I realised that I couldn't go through with it." She felt herself blushing even more as she lied her way back to him.

"So, what you just slept in the same hotel and nothing happened?" His question was scathing. Who ever heard of lying to your husband and booking separate rooms?

She hesitated slightly. "No … like I said, I couldn't go through with it. I left and went to the premier inn. I couldn't come home because I'd told you I was with Maria."

He frowned and the knot of worry in Josie's stomach twisted painfully. "But you must have been drinking … with dinner … and probably lunch? How could you have driven?"

Josie felt her face burning with embarrassment at the memory of her recklessness. Who was that woman who appeared to have overtaken her mind and body? Drink driving went against everything she believed in. She had instilled it into her kids, terrified that they would kill themselves or their friends or end up in jail.

"I know … " she said quietly, "Like I said, I think I may have lost my mind."

"Jesus." Trevor sighed loudly. "Thank god nothing happened."

"I know." Josie's face was grim. "I go over and over it in my mind, thinking of all of the other ways that that journey could have ended. But …"

"But?"

"But at least I came to my senses and got away before I did anything equally as stupid."

There was a long silence, which Trevor eventually broke.

"So, have you stayed in touch with him?"

Josie was shaking her head but her reassurance was interrupted as they both looked up suddenly, distracted by flashing lights lit up outside their bedroom window. Trevor stood up and moved away from her to look. "Ambulance." he stated grimly. "Outside Cynthia's"

"Oh god." Much as she disliked the woman, Josie immediately feared that her neighbour may be the latest victim of Covid 19. Cynthia was probably mid-fifties and carrying a bit of weight. Covid had proven to be no friend to the obese.

They were quiet for a while. They didn't like to spy but couldn't help but watch as the paramedics carefully donned their PPE and went solemnly into their neighbour's home.

"No, I haven't" Josie answered his question now, wanting to put the whole sorry tale behind her. "Trevor, I am so so sorry. I have been a complete fool. I honestly thought that I was dying and I know it's no excuse, but I just ..."

He looked at her thoughtfully. "I think you might need to see a doctor, Josie."

"What do you mean?" her voice was panicky.

"Well ... it's not normal to believe that you are dying just from reading your bloody horoscope!" He wished he could laugh. If someone told him this about their wife he would be howling. But somehow, it just wasn't funny.

"Chapter Twenty Seven

One of the weird things about 2020 was how quickly time seemed to pass by, in spite of the fact that most people had done very little other than work and worry. Another week disappeared and England found itself in the most incomprehensible of lockdowns. Pubs, restaurants, hairdressers, gyms and the like were all closed. People were not allowed to mix with anyone outside of their households apart from with one other person for outdoor exercise. But apparently it was safe for schools and universities to be open, for show homes to be open and people could visit a house that was for sale but could not visit their family. Hannah and Harry were not allowed home and a family Christmas looked like a fantasy not likely to happen. Josie and Trevor came to the end of their self-isolation period and were busy re-kindling the love that had held them together for so long. They had slow, leisurely walks where they held hands and hardly spoke but enjoyed a sense of tranquillity, listening to only the sound of the birds and the wind in the trees.

Josie had had a shock when Trevor had suggested that she see a doctor. Did he think she was insane?

"You don't need to be insane to have a mental health issue." Trevor had reassured her. "I just think that you have been suffering in silence and you need some support."

And so she had taken the bull by the horns and phoned the doctors. It was hard. Now, more than ever the receptionists seemed to think it was ok to ask what the problem was, screening every call to try to minimise the number of people visiting the surgery. It had taken a few days before she spoke to a GP but when she did, she was honest about her anxiety. The GP had commented that she was not on her own during such unprecedented times and this helped a little to persuade Josie that she was not going mad or had become the village idiot. He had put her in touch with a counsellor and incredibly, she had an appointment lined up for the following week. She had heard so much about waiting lists for mental health issues but by all accounts the surgery had invested in their own in-house counsellor and there had been a cancellation slot that she was able to take.

"We seem to be keeping counsellors in business anyway." Josie had remarked to her husband tentatively.

Trevor had been quiet for a while but eventually had spoken seriously. "I think ..... no, I know... " he stated emphatically, "that it's me who got that all wrong."

They had not spoken about Harry other than to worry about him being so far away from home during the global pandemic. They had not mentioned the unmentionable. Josie did not respond but felt her heart skip a beat.

Trevor cleared his throat. "I'm not saying I've got it all sorted in my head."

Josie had squeezed his arm reassuringly and he continued.

"But, I realise that I've been very wrong. I've been doing some research and I realise that it's not a choice he's making. It's just how he's made." He hesitated. "How we made him."

Josie had wrapped her arms around him and pulled him towards her. It was her turn now to reassure him.

"You just need time," she said gently.

"I know. I am so glad he doesn't know how I reacted." Suddenly his eyes had filled with panic.

"He doesn't does he?"

"No! No, of course not." Josie smiled. "I love you both too much to cause that kind of trouble."

Chapter Twenty Eight

Another week came and went. A week that saw Donald Trump toppled as President of the United States of America. He was to be replaced by the septuagenarian, Joe Biden, leaving the nation divided and the Trump camp bitterly claiming that the result had been fraudulently achieved.

"Maybe it's an omen that normality is returning." Trevor had mused optimistically.

"Don't count on it." Josie had responded, thinking of the 50,000 people who had now died from the disease in the UK alone. The news that week that a vaccine was now imminent was doing little to quell Josie's nerves. 50,000 families' lives had been torn apart. The victims of the virus were not all elderly or obese, "normal" people had died and she could have been one of them, still could be. The effects of "long covid" were now being discovered and Josie herself was yet to return to full health. She was trying to rebuild her strength but short and slow walks were all that she could manage and even if the gym were open, she doubted that she would have the energy for a return to her pre-covid routine.

Josie had had her first session with her counsellor and discovered that the anxiety had been creeping up on her for a long time, even prior to the onset of the global pandemic. The counsellor had explained how it was often the case that there was a build up over time and the signs were not always obvious.

She had given her some breathing exercises to do and some videos to watch to help her "reframe unhelpful thoughts" and "tackle worries." She had also emphasised the importance of healthy diet, exercise and sleep, all of which had been affected by the turmoil in Josie's life in the preceding months.

It was all well and good to try to manage her mind, thought Josie, but how did you stop worrying about your kids? When do you stop worrying about your kids? She thought of the years ahead that for a while she had convinced herself she wouldn't have.

"Why did no one tell you that having children was a life sentence of worry?" she pondered out loud to Trevor.

"Hey, come on Jose, it's not like anything would have stopped you from wanting a family." Trevor had reasoned.

"I know, you're right." she had conceded with a smile, thinking back to finding out that she was pregnant for the first time. She had rushed out to buy every parenting magazine she could lay her hands on and had drank in all the new information with an unquenchable thirst to become the best mother she could be.

That evening, she had expected Trevor to have golf on TV as it was the Masters and Trevor was addicted so she had an evening planned with her Kindle. To her surprise Trevor was not watching the golf when she went into the living room after finishing clearing the kitchen. The TV was paused and he got up as she came in. "Give me a sec" he said with a mischievous grin. She heard the clink of glasses and then to her surprise the pop of a cork. Trevor was not a fan of prosecco; if ever he was deviating from a good old pint, he would be a red wine man. He came in a few minutes later holding two flutes, one of which he offered her.

"Thank you! I didn't think you liked prosecco?"

"I don't. It's not prosecco." He clinked his glass against hers. "To us." He toasted.

"To us." she echoed and took a sip. "Champagne! What's this in aid of?"

"In aid of living for the day ... and me celebrating my lovely wife and family .... Thank you."

She watched as he put his glass down and went over to the TV. He bent down and baffled, she watched him fiddling with the ancient video recorder that was never used now that they had Netflix.

As the first image came on the screen, she realised what he was up to. "Aw Trevor, what about the golf?"

"What about it?" He smiled before picking his glass back up and settling down beside her. For the next three hours, they watched the old home-made videos of their two children. They laughed and cried and exclaimed in surprise as long-forgotten memories re-played themselves out in front of them. Hannah's first steps and Harry falling headfirst into the paddling pool, Hannah beaming on her tricycle and Harry carefully putting his teddy to bed after he had read him a story and kissed him good night.

"I'm such an idiot." Trevor had said quietly. "How did I not see it?"

"You don't have to be gay to be caring." Jodie had said lightly.

"I know but the signs were there, weren't they?"

"I know …I didn't see it either, remember."

He paused thoughtfully. "Do you think Erin guessed?"

Josie had given it some thought on more than one occasion. "I kind of hope so. It's not the kind of bombshell you want to hear from someone you're in love with is it?"

"At least they will remain friends, no nastiness or anything. She's such a lovely girl" Trevor couldn't keep the sadness out of his voice and Josie squeezed his hand lovingly.

"He will meet someone else lovely. He just needs time. I hope he doesn't meet anyone over there and end up locked up."

"He's too sensible to do anything stupid even if he does meet someone."

Josie felt a surge of love for her husband. It sounded as though he had finally accepted their son's homosexuality.

"Oh god, this bloody year!" She exclaimed "Let's book a holiday!"

"We don't need to go on holiday to enjoy ourselves." Trevor grabbed her, pulling her towards him. Before she could speak, he has swept her up into his arms.

"What are you doing?" Josie squealed with shock and delight as he lifted her and carried her giggling up the stairs.

Chapter Twenty Nine

Josie woke with a heavy head but smiled to herself as she remembered the previous evening. She rolled over and realised that Trevor was not at her side. She picked up her phone and scrolled down the news items. It was so depressing. The UK daily death rate was now back to what it had been in May and yet there will still reports of illegal raves and gatherings with some people literally appearing to believe that they were immune to the deadly disease.

Trevor came into the bedroom carrying a tray with drinks and delicious smelling croissants.

Josie was delighted. "Mmmm that smells..." she was about to say delicious but she stopped when she saw Trevor's serious expression. Immediately, she thought of their two children and she asked him what was wrong as sick panic filled her stomach.

He set the tray down on the bed. "Don't panic." He hesitated.

"Has something happened to one of the kids?" Josie was gripped with fear.

"No." Trevor replied hurriedly. "It's not us. It's Cynthia"

"Cynthia?"

"She's gone. Passed away." Trevor's expression was grim. "I just saw whatshisname next door when I popped to get the croissants."

"You've been out? Sorry, stupid question." She knew they hadn't had any fresh croissants in the cupboard. "God, I'm so confused. So … was it Covid?"

Trevor nodded grimly.

Josie was overwhelmed with sadness. "Poor, poor woman. Oh my god, when will this nightmare be over?"

"When we get the vaccine hopefully." Trevor responded flatly.

To her own and Trevor's surprise, Josie burst into tears.

Trevor pulled her toward him and kissed the top of her head.

"What's the matter with me?" Josie gulped in between sobs.

"It's the anxiety, love. Your emotions are all over the place."

"I don't deserve you."

"True!" Trevor hugged her. "I'm joking." He kissed her gently. "Can you manage a croissant?"

Josie looked at him apologetically. "I'm sorry, I don't think I can at the moment. Could we go for a walk first, maybe? I just need to get out of the house. I feel as though I'm going mad."

Within fifteen minutes they were in the car, driving toward one of Josie's favourite spots. It was a cold and windy day but at least, Josie commented, it made you feel alive to have the wind in your face.

They sat on a bench after walking for almost an hour and revelled in the autumn colours. Josie closed her eyes and listened to the wind in the trees and the birds, not even the remotest hint of the chaos that consumed the country or indeed the world.

A rustling sound brought her out of her reverie and she laughed as for the second time that morning, Trevor offered her a croissant.

"You are a life saver. Literally. I'm starving." Josie wolfed down two croissants. Not as warm as they were when first offered a couple of hours ago but still delicious. "I love you Trevor Winters."

"I love you too." She tasted the butter on his lips and thanked god that her stupidity had been short lived. But the death of her neighbour had shocked her and she realised that there was another missing link in her life. It wasn't just her children that she was missing. She missed her friend. So much.

Chapter Thirty

Christmas 2020 was now just a month away. The country had waited with baited breath to hear Boris's Christmas plan. It was eventually announced that there would be a four day window from 23 until 27 December when families would be able to enjoy Christmas. Families could form a bubble with two other households which was fine if you were a nuclear family with young children, and just one set of parents each but pretty much a non-starter for the millions of "blended" families around the country. Maria watched the announcement with a heavy heart. The year had been the worst since she had met Mark and back in the summer when social distancing outdoors had made lockdown bearable, she had looked forward to a family Christmas with life returning to a new normal. The new normal for them was living with Mark's condition, the constant reminder that he was now "clinically vulnerable" and the dread that he would become a covid statistic. She had greeted the news of the vaccine success and the fact that there was light at the end of that particular tunnel with trepidation. Some reports stated that those with the weakest immune systems should not have it whilst others said they would be first in line. How were they supposed to know what or who to believe?

Mark himself remained astonishingly optimistic. He had continued to work during the second lockdown in which schools had remained open.

After a lengthy discussion with his headteacher and extra measures put in place to protect him, he was happy to be able to continue to do the job that he loved. No one could have foreseen a day when teenagers would be walking around school in face masks but whilst it was evident that some were traumatised by the lockdown experience when they had been learning from home for four long months, most of them failed to understand the concept of social distancing. How could you expect them to understand that they had to stay two metres apart in the corridor when they were sat next to each other in the classroom? Mark was as keen as anyone that they limit the mental impact of isolation and home learning upon young people and so he forced himself to quash his own qualms in relation to his condition. In front of Maria he was relentlessly positive but there were moments when he felt secretly afraid. He loved his life, he didn't want it to be curtailed.

He managed to get home early on the Friday following the announcement of the Christmas restrictions . By the time Maria had arrived home from work the house was lit up with the Christmas lights and the garden adorned with her favourite illuminated ornaments.

He wished he could see Maria's face as she rounded the corner to see their home, which along with a number of their neighbours had now truly entered into the Christmas spirit, stubbornly standing up to the Covid crisis. She came through the door laughing. "You always said we weren't allowed to put them up until December!" she exclaimed happily as he swept her into his arms.

"Well some rules are meant to be broken." He kissed her gently. "We'll go and get a tree tomorrow. The weather's going to be rubbish so we will stay nice and cosy once we've fetched it. I can even see some mulled wine coming on."

"Absolutely." Maria joined in the Christmas spirit. "And it's never too early to start on the mince pies."

He handed her a glass of red wine and she took a slow sip, allowing the warmth to spread through her body. She sighed. "Next year everything should be back to normal and we will have a new little person in the family." She was so excited. Their first grandchild was due in the spring; so impatient was she to have a baby in the family, it was almost a physical ache.

Mark sensed her need to be surrounded by people. They had always had weekly family get-togethers with their children and Maria was very much a sociable being who loved to be serving up food, dancing in the kitchen and generally just being with others. He hesitated before broaching the subject of the rift with her friend.

"Have you been in touch with Josie at all?"

Maria shook her head. She missed her friend badly. Even in the original lockdown, they had communicated at least weekly and they had helped to keep each other sane at an insane time. She found herself wondering almost daily how things had turned out between her and Trevor. She was fond of Trevor too and hated to think of him being hurt. She still felt incensed by her friend's stupidity and recklessness. She couldn't believe that she would risk her marriage, her family unity for a fling.

"I do keep thinking of her," She responded quietly. "of them really. I hope they are ok. But I'm still really angry with her. I know it's not my place to judge but … I don't know … Trevor is just such a decent guy, he would never hurt her."

"No one knows what goes on in a marriage though, Maria. She must have had her reasons."

"Humph!" Maria was scathing. "Boredom, that's all it was. Just bloody boredom. Well, we all get bored sometimes."

"Thanks!" Mark interjected with mock indignation.

She pulled him towards her. "You know what I mean. Sometimes you have to make an effort, don't you?"

"Well, I never have to try very hard to want you." He kissed her on the mouth, enjoying the taste of the wine on her lips.

"I am so lucky to have found you!"

"You are!" He laughed but was suddenly serious. "Why don't you give her a call? You've been friends for so long and life's too short."

She didn't want to think about his last statement; it scared her too much. But he was right, she realised. They had been through thick and thin together and maybe she had been too harsh, too judgemental. Suddenly she felt panicked, it was a strange sensation that she had felt more and more often of late, a feeling of dread that something awful was going to happen. This bloody virus had messed her head up.

"Do you know what?" she announced determinedly. "I will do it now! Well, I'll text at least. It's less intrusive; do you agree?"

"I agree!" He concurred happily.

Chapter Thirty One

Josie was cooking in the kitchen. The radio was playing non-stop Christmas songs and she couldn't make up her mind whether she was enjoying them or was irritated by them. She heard her phone ping but was in the middle of stirring vegetables in the wok and so she made a mental note to check it as soon as possible. She was taking the food through to the dining room a short while later when she saw the message icon lit up on her phone. She almost dropped the wok.

"Text from Maria" her phone informed her.

"Oh my god!" She was shaking as she quickly deposited the pan on the table and hurried back to pick up the message. It was quite brief but the tone was apologetic and friendly.

"Hello Josie, I hope you are all ok and staying safe at this horrible time? I am sorry I haven't been in touch and haven't been there for you. I hope you have sorted things out with Trev … I was thinking we could catch up soon ….? Love Maria xxx"

Josie felt herself consumed with happiness, seeing her friend extending the olive branch. Trevor was bringing in the wine and noticed her jittery state. He threw her a questioning look.

"Text from Maria"

Trevor didn't know whether this was good or bad and paused mid wine corking.

Josie clasped her hand to her mouth and nodded. "It's good. She's just asking how we are, but it's good, Trev, so good!"

Trevor placed the wine bottle on the table and caught his wife as she collapsed into his arms, sobbing.

"I've been such an idiot." She could hardly get her breath.

"If I had a pound for every time you've said that recently ..."

"I didn't realise what I had. I nearly lost everything ... you ... Maria"

"Stop it." Trevor was firm. "You didn't , you haven't. I love you. Maria loves you. Come on, let's eat and then you can reply to Maria. Everything is going to be ok."

"Promise?" Josie knew it was a stupid question. No one knew the answer to that.

* * *

"Hello"

Josie closed her eyes, drinking in the delicious sound of her friend's familiar voice. They both started speaking at the same time and then simultaneously dissolved into nervous laughter.

"You first."

"No you." Maria's voice was firm and Josie knew that Maria had the right to the upper hand. Josie had gone up to the bedroom. She'd asked Trevor if he minded and he hesitated only slightly before assuring her that it was ok. They had always loved their girly chats and he knew that whatever had happened, he could trust his wife once more. Josie settled back into the pillows on her bed.

"Ok." Josie said softly. "Maria, I am so sorry." She paused, overwhelmed with the idea that she could win her friendship back. She heard Maria take a heavy breath and she panicked, not knowing what was going through her friend's mind, not knowing if she could even call her her friend. "I've been an idiot." She added hurriedly.

"True." Maria was not beating around the bush. If they were going to clear the air, they needed to be honest with each other. She needed to be sure that Josie really did regret the way that she had behaved but she also needed to understand what had been going on for her to risk throwing away her marriage and their friendship.

Josie was grateful for her friend's honesty. "Where to begin ..." she pondered.

"Well, you could start by telling me where you had been when you told Trev you were with me?" Maria tried hard to keep her tone gentle.

"Oh god, I am so sorry Maria. I really am."

"Ok," Maria was impatient with all of the apologies, "stop apologising and start explaining." She demanded with an air of authority.

"I ended up on my own in a Premier Inn, thank goodness. I didn't go through with the madness. I couldn't." Josie cringed visibly at the white lie – or was it simply a lie – she was glad they were not video calling.

"Soooo, where did you start off?" Maria enquired, baffled.

And so Josie told her the pitiful tale of how infatuated she had become and truthfully described the fun day she had had with Jeff. She couldn't bring herself to tell her the truth about how pathetic he had looked, dribbling and asleep. She realised ironically that it was the type of story that would have had them howling with laughter had they heard it about someone else. She had told Trevor a version of events that she repeated now. She wanted so much for that to be the version that was true that she almost believed it herself.

"Well," Maria stated emphatically when Josie had finished. "At least you came to your senses before too much damage was done."

"I know," Josie responded ruefully, "although I had a few pretty rough weeks with Trevor threatening to divorce me."

"Really?" Maria was all ears. "Well good for him at least it shows he's got some backbone. Let's face it, would you really want to be with someone who was a pushover? Good old Trev. He is such a lovely, honest man you know, Josie."

"I know."

"And I know things can get boring sometimes but . . ."

Josie interrupted. "Well, that's the only good thing to come out of it!"

"Tell me more!" Maria giggled, wide eyed.

"Well, let's just say Trev's had a new lease of life." She laughed coyly. "And what with us being empty nesters ...mmmm," she murmured deliciously, " I didn't realise my husband still had such energy."

Maria felt a sudden stab of sorrow as she reflected how her own husband seemed to tire so much more easily these days. She let out an involuntary sigh.

There was a short silence before Josie, sensing something was not quite right, asked if everything was ok.

Maria had not intended to share her bad news. It was not the kind of news that should be delivered by phone. She hesitated and decided that now was not the time.

"Look, why don't we go for a walk or something next week."

"Are we allowed?" Josie was trying to keep up with the Covid rules, but it was difficult. The second national lockdown was due to end but the tier system would resume and their area was expected to be in the highest tier, meaning that pubs and restaurants would remain shut and no mixing outside of the household was allowed.

"I haven't got a clue." Maria's voice was flat, which was unlike her. "But, I'm just talking a walk over Cannock Chase; we won't face the firing squad for that will we?" She was referring to a local beauty spot that appeared to be permanently peopled with walkers and cyclists even during the coldest weather now that families no longer had the option of ambling around shopping centres.

"I shouldn't think so." Josie was ecstatic at the prospect of seeing her friend and then suddenly realised that they had missed so much of each other's news in the past few months. "Oh my god, I haven't told you! I had Covid!"

Maria's stomach somersaulted. She had to protect her husband. "When?" she asked tentatively, mentally already backtracking on her suggestion of a walk.

"Oh it was weeks ago now." Josie sensed something not quite right in her friend's response. "I'm the safest person you could wish to meet right now, positively fizzing with antibodies."

"I'm sorry. I didn't mean to be so insensitive. God, Jose, was it awful?" She felt a sudden sense of panic. This virus was a killer. Dear god, what if something terrible had happened and they had not made up ... Tears slid silently down her face. 2020 had been one hell of a bloody year. And it wasn't over yet, the year or the virus, Maria reflected ruefully.

"It was pretty awful, yes." admitted Josie, remembering the desolate days, contemplating what was going to be worse ... death or divorce ... However, she was conscious that she had dominated the conversation with her woes and triumphs. She had heard very little of Maria's experiences over recent months. "Are you ok, Maria?"

"Yes, yes, don't worry about me. Ok, let's see what the weather's doing next week and we'll go and get some vitamin D?"

"Absolutely." Josie was warm with the joy of being reunited with her friend. "And Maria ..."

"Yes?"

"Thank you." Josie was choked. Notwithstanding the ongoing Covid nightmare, she felt as though she was getting her life back.

Chapter Thirty Two

Josie was singing along to "Driving home for Christmas" on her way back from her Christmas shop. She was weary from trying to socially distance, mask wearing and struggling to see through steamed up glasses. 2020 had brought some concepts that, previously alien, now had just become the norm. There were just two days until the big day. It was certainly going to be a different type of Christmas this year. The last couple of weeks had seen the Covid numbers as bad as they had been in the spring, with over 700 people losing their life according to the latest daily statistics and if things were not as dire and depressing already, there was now news of a new strain of the virus, which transmitted with even more alarming alacrity than the original. "V" Day earlier in the month had brought short-lived euphoria for in spite of the fact that the first vaccines outside of clinical trials had been administered, it was clear that there were going to be issues with storage and supply before the general population would be receiving the long awaited jab. The government was also up against a serious effort by "anti vaxxers" to undermine and discredit the injection, with social media erupting amidst claims that likened the drug to thalidomide and conspiracy theories that claimed that people would be simultaneously implanted with a tracking microchip.

In addition to the rising panic of a "no deal Brexit", the government also had to race against the clock to get lorry drivers tested in order to re-open the border with France, whose president, himself a victim of Covid 19, had decreed it unsafe for trade to continue with the risks of transmission so high. Schools had been shocked to hear third hand that the new January term would see a staggered return, with many schools already broken up for the festive break before headteachers were made officially aware of the latest, ever-changing guidelines.

Josie herself was again working from home, which suited her fine if she were honest but nevertheless, she was happy to have finished now for a week or so. She had spent the day cleaning and intermittently chatting with Hannah and Harry, who had returned for the Christmas break, albeit that they were in "Tier 3", which meant that all bars and restaurants were shut, so they were all going to be celebrating at home. The plan to allow a window of four days when households could form a "bubble of three" had been dispensed with earlier that week and now families were allowed to meet with a maximum of two other households on Christmas Day only. The introduction of a fourth tier had meant that much of the country was locked down completely. It was difficult some days to remain positive but for Josie, having her children home safe and well was more than she could have wished for. Trevor's mom, Moira, had decided that the safest thing was to stay at home and so Josie was planning to take her her three course meal round on a tray. Josie's own parents, although ten years younger than Moira, were equally cautious and said they didn't feel safe meeting people indoors, especially with Hannah and Harry having been out in the big wide world recently. Trevor had had the genius idea of erecting outdoor heaters around his decking area but the current torrential rain meant that their plans to sit outside were looking extremely precarious.

Harry was there on the drive when she pulled up, ready to help her unload the car and fill the fridge. She had missed him so much.

"Where's Hannah?"

Harry frowned, "Not sure actually, I've been on the laptop, wasn't paying much attention."

Josie called up to her daughter but on receiving no reply, she went up to her room. Josie found her fast asleep, curled up in the foetal position, clutching her childhood teddy. Josie crept back out. Hannah had been sleeping a lot in the week or so since her return. Josie couldn't help worrying as fatigue was one of the signs of Covid 19. Hannah had been insisting that she was fine and didn't need to be tested for the virus.

"Just too much partying!" She was being ironic of course, there had been no partying for students this year and much of the tuition so far had been on line. "I'm joking, mom." She added impatiently,

"It's just so difficult to sleep when you've been cooped up in the same room for hours on end."

"Are you getting any exercise?" Josie had enquired tentatively.

Hannah had given her a look. "Yes, mom, I have been exercising and eating and not drinking too much." She hadn't been back five minutes before the familiar exasperated tone had returned but Josie ignored it. She was still only eighteen years old. She might think she was grown up but grown ups knew better.

She went back down to Harry who was putting the last of the Christmas goodies in the fridge.

"Crikey, mom," he commented, surveying the array of treats, "You have remembered that we can't have people round haven't you?"

Josie sighed, "I know, but it's hard; I'm just trying to make it feel as normal as possible."

"We'll have a good day, mom." Harry said brightly. "I'm just glad to be home."

"And I am absolutely so glad to have you home, my darling." Josie gave her son a big, long hug. She hadn't even asked him when he was due back. She couldn't bear the thought of him returning to Dubai. Way back in August when he had left, they thought that the worst of the virus was behind them and that life would be back to normal by now. No one would have guessed that it would be worse than ever. Their excited thoughts of joining their son for a holiday had gradually faded as holiday plans for the early part of 2021 at least remained on hold. He had looked worried when he had first greeted them, looking hesitantly at his father. Josie had tried to reassure him that his dad had accepted him being gay but he had to see it with his own eyes and hear it for himself.

The opportunity presented itself on Christmas Eve. Josie had gone for a leisurely bath and pamper. "I need to do my own nails this year." She had grumbled.

"Er … Mom!" Harry had responded sternly, silently admonishing her for lamenting the loss of her luxury when many had lost so much more.

"I know." Josie acknowledged, "But to be fair, I have had Covid so you'd think I'd be entitled to a Christmas manicure." She had looked at their blank faces and retreated rapidly to her bedroom, where she had a candle wafting out evening lavender and white birch, promising a state of relaxation and calm.

Trevor had shaken his head and raised his eyes to the ceiling, "Women!" he tutted and then quickly feared that he might be offending his son, by implying that they both had the same "problem".

Harry noted his look of alarm. "It's ok, dad, you don't have to tread on eggshells."

Trevor looked embarrassed.

"I'm still the same person." Harry continued with a note of desperation. He needed to know that his father still felt the same about him. He had always been so proud of him. Losing that would be unbearable for Harry.

Trevor cleared his throat awkwardly. "I know, Harry. I do know that." He looked his son fully in the eye. For his part, he needed him to know that he still loved him as he had always done. "I can't deny that I found it very difficult at first ... you know ... when your mom told me." His face reddened self-consciously. He was ashamed of his initial reaction now that months had passed and so much, but also so little, had happened since he had waved his son goodbye. Suddenly, he wanted to be honest with his son. He didn't want them to have secrets from each other any longer. He had always wanted to be the kind of father that his kids could talk to but, clearly, he had failed there.

"You look sad, dad." Harry observed quietly. He felt a sense of panic at the thought that his father had not accepted the situation after all. "I'm so sorry if I've disappointed you." Harry's voice broke and he realised that he was crying. "I.. I can't help it ..." he faltered. "I did try ... you know ... to love Erin ... in that way... but I just couldn't ... It's not who I am."

"Jesus, Harry!" Trevor now too was crying and he leapt out of his seat to envelope his son in a massive bear hug. "You could never disappoint me." He held him so close, Harry started to cough and they both ended up laughing through shared, salty, snotty tears. Trevor quashed the memory of his disappointment and he was engulfed with shame. He needed to confess, he needed the catharsis and a fresh start with his son. "I had to have counselling."

The words tumbled out and lay themselves bare. Harry was momentarily shocked. So, his mom had lied, his dad hadn't accepted it as readily as she had made out. But Harry was wise beyond his years and he was a glass half full type of person.

"But dad, that's amazing!"

"Is it?" Trevor was confused.

"Yes!" Harry was excited as the notion revealed itself to himself as he spoke. "Because you found it hard but you loved me enough to accept help! It's amazing, thank you so much."

Trevor scratched his head. Wow, what a generous way of looking at it. He really didn't deserve such a loving and forgiving son. He shook his head and wiped away his tears gruffly. "Thank you, Harry," Again, he hugged his son to him. "I don't deserve you."

"Probably not!" Harry smiled.

Trevor smiled, genuinely glowing with pride as he looked at his son. "You know, at least this goddamn Covid business has made people, me included, start to count their blessings. Life is so precious and can be taken from you so quickly. The most important thing is to be honest with each other and to accept people for who they are."

Harry nodded his agreement and he started to glimpse a happier future where he could be himself with the people he cared most about. There had been so many years when he had felt a sense of inner turmoil and fear of an uncertain future. There was something else he needed to tell his parents but that could wait until tomorrow.

Chapter Thirty Three

Christmas Day was certainly going to be different but Josie awoke early to hear the birds singing and the promise of a cold but dry and sunny day. After days of rain, which saw serious flooding in some areas of the country, it seemed that at last something was going right. Josie's parents had finally agreed to pop round briefly, weather permitting, during mid morning so Josie attempted to get Hannah and Harry up around eight thirty. She recalled the years of early morning present opening and the excitement that was always palpable as the children used to rush downstairs to check whether "he had been". Now, she struggled to get them out of bed, even with the smell of freshly cooked bacon and eggs to tempt them downstairs. By the time their grandparents had arrived, they were washed and showered but their presents were yet to be opened. Trevor had pre-heated the heaters in the garden and despite the freezing temperature, they managed an hour in the garden exchanging gifts and pleasantries with family that they had barely spent any time with in the preceding nine months. Mike and Helen were visibly nervous and there were none of the usual Christmas hugs but Josie did manage to convince them that they would be perfectly safe having a mug of hot chocolate with them. "The cups have been in the dishwasher and my hands are sanitised." She assured them brightly but she was saddened by the fear that this disease had instilled into the elderly and the vulnerable. Gifts this year were somewhat restrained as last year's trips and vouchers remained yet to be enjoyed so there was little point in spending more money on events that could not be guaranteed.

Josie and Trevor made a joint effort in preparing the dinner and Josie loaded the boot of her car with the goodies that they had bought for her mother-in-law, as well as the plates of food. Moira was in good spirits in spite of spending the day alone. She had mastered the art of WhatsApp video calling and so she didn't feel entirely isolated. Back home, Josie had what she felt was a much-deserved glass of prosecco and the family sat together in the dining room, raising their glasses to wish each other a merry Christmas. Trevor had brought Josie up to speed with his heart to heart with his son as they lay in bed on Christmas Eve and Josie had caressed her husband gently, as once again tears fell whilst he related the candid conversation. She noted during their Christmas meal that the atmosphere between father and son was just as it had always been. All's well that ends well, she had told herself contentedly, sipping her prosecco and surveying her family. Thank goodness, they were all back together, safe and sound. Never, ever again, would she jeopardise this family. She shuddered involuntarily as she recalled her crazy behaviour. She looked at each member of her family in turn, her heart filled with love for them. Her gaze rested on Hannah, who she now noticed was looking pale, with shadows under her beautiful blue eyes. She was pushing her food around her plate, clearly struggling. Josie frowned, remembering that she had hardly touched her breakfast either. It was not like Hannah, who normally had a hearty appetite. Nevertheless, Josie was happy that their chatter over lunch was bright and optimistic; in recent days Boris had finally secured a Brexit deal and in spite of further strains of the virus being discovered in various global locations, there was a great deal of positivity surrounding the vaccines that were now being hailed as successful and had started to be rolled out.

For the first time in many years, there had been no preview of the Queen's speech and so after dinner, they sat together to watch and listen to what their long-reigning monarch would have to say about a very unique year. They all had a tear in their eye as they listened to the ninety four year old assure the nation that they were "not alone", when so many had spent so long isolated from friends and family.

"Oh dear, let's hope next year is better." Josie had had a few Proseccos by now and was feeling sentimental. "Shall we play a game? Or watch a film together?"

"Home alone!" voted Harry, it had always been his favourite and when he was five years old, he had known practically every line. Josie remembered how she had been horrified when he was given the film by a family friend; she had been convinced that he would be traumatised for life. As usual, she was completely wrong; he had loved it and had watched it over and over. They had all been horrified but in stitches when months later, he had bellowed "Keep the change, you filthy animal!" through the letter box to the pizza delivery man. It turned out that he hadn't even really wanted pizza, he had just wanted to use his much-rehearsed line in real life. Josie, bright red, had opened the door, apologised and quickly taken the pizzas, ironically urging him to, in fact , keep the change.

No one had any argument with the much-loved film and they settled down to watch it together. Hannah was the first to fall asleep and Josie felt a twinge of worry return as she looked at her daughter, who, in sleep, looked as pretty as ever but she clearly wasn't herself.

Later that night, Josie slipped into bed beside her husband. She shuddered and cuddled into Trevor. She had been trying to heed the government's advice to keep windows open in a bid to blow the virus out. She herself might have survived the virus but there was no room for complacency and no one was certain that you couldn't have it more than once.

"Thank you for my lovely gifts." She kissed her husband's shoulder sleepily as she snuggled into him. They had agreed that they would not buy each other much under the circumstances and she had been delighted with the expensive perfume set and beautiful earrings that he had presented her with earlier in the day.

Trevor reached under the pillow. "Well, the day's not over yet. Merry Christmas" He whispered softly as he handed her an envelope.

"What's this?" Josie exclaimed, sitting up, surprised.

"I realised that I needed to make up for your rubbish birthday present." He answered sheepishly referring to the vacuum cleaner that he had foolishly thought was the answer to a girl's dreams.

Suddenly wide awake, she opened the envelope with a sense of intrigue.

"Thank you!" She exclaimed happily as she read the small print. Trevor had arranged for the two of them to go on a river cruise along the Danube the following August. "How romantic! I love you Trevor Winters."

Trevor beamed happily. "I love you too Josie Winters. Next year will be so much better." He declared optimistically. "I booked August as this bloody Covid nonsense should be all sorted by then."

"I'll be fifty!" Josie exclaimed as if she had only just realised that the milestone birthday was now less than six months away.

"But still fantastic!" Trevor muttered and drew her to him, enveloping her with his body and a long, loving kiss.

Chapter Thirty Four

The bright, crisp weather of Christmas day was short-lived and Boxing Day made a misty and miserable appearance. A few days after Christmas they woke to quite a heavy snowfall, much to their surprise and Josie's irritation. She wanted to be out and about, going for long walks; she was conscious that she still had not managed the walk with Maria due to the busy pre-Christmas period and the wet weather. They had remained in contact almost daily however and their former closeness seemed to have resumed. Their friendship appeared firmly in tact, leaving Josie feeling relieved and blessed. On Christmas day, believing the dry weather would last, they had made a provisional arrangement to meet up mid-way between Christmas and New Year.

"It's so annoying." Josie was moaning via text to Maria, referring to the snow.

"It's so pretty!" Maria had responded more positively. "Let's get wrapped up and meet at the park. It'll be lovely over there, with all the trees and the lake will look so beautiful."

Josie was not a walking in the snow type of person, but she was desperate to meet up with her friend in the flesh and so had readily agreed.

Hannah was having a lazy morning pampering herself and she had uni work to tackle. The men were quite content to stay in and watch football, so

Josie made herself and Maria hot chocolate in portable cups and set off to meet her friend, with a flutter of excited butterflies in her stomach.

They laughed as they walked towards each other at the entrance to the park, each noticing that the other had had the same idea and carried two hot drinks.

"Not to worry," Maria said cheerfully, "You can never have too much of a good thing."

Josie agreed and they "air hugged", which had become the new normal, in line with social distancing. The park was quite busy and they were passed by multiple cyclists and joggers. Most people were wearing masks and so they felt as safe as they could in the circumstances. They chatted initially about the weather, Covid figures, which were alarming, with further restrictions expected to be announced imminently and how they had celebrated their Christmas within the constraints imposed upon them.

"I've been so spoilt, this year." Josie informed her friend happily. "I really don't deserve Trevor, do I?" she added guiltily.

"Well, no." Maria conceded before giving her a playful push. "Oops, sorry, social distancing." she added, hurriedly withdrawing. They walked in silence for a few moments before Maria spoke again. "Seriously, are you two ok now? I was worried about you, you know, both of you."

"Honestly," Josie assured her emphatically, "We have never been better. I have told myself a million times what an idiot I was, believe me, I'll never forgive myself."

"You must." Maria stated firmly but kindly. "Everyone is entitled to make a mistake, Josie."

Josie sighed quietly, "I know. And … I know it's no excuse but I honestly think I was having some kind of mental breakdown."

"It's this bloody virus." Maria replied with a note of despair. "So many mental health worries, Mark says it's awful at school. It's not normal to be isolated for so long. Some kids didn't see anyone other than their own household for four months at least, longer in some cases, because of the six weeks holiday, so, effectively from March to September." She shook her head, it was incomprehensible, something no one could have predicted. "Some kids barely speak now, they are so anxious, especially if they have someone clinically vulnerable in their family." Her voice tailed off and Josie realised to her alarm that tears had filled her friend's eyes. She stopped in her tracks.

"God, Maria, are you ok?" She was filled with panic. Was Maria just being emotional about the general awfulness of the pandemic or was there something else …

Maria sniffed and fished a pack of tissues out of her pocket. "Would you mind if we sat down for a few moments?" She pointed to a nearby bench.

"Of course not." Josie's stomach was in knots, worrying about her friend.

They sat at opposite ends of the bench – hardly conducive to the sensitive conversation that Maria was about to broach.

"Just after the first lockdown," Maria began quietly. Josie was struggling to hear and found herself leaning towards her friend. She placed the cups she was carrying beside her and reached instinctively for her face mask. Maria was instantly grateful and did the same. She started at the beginning and told her friend the shocking news of the cancer that now resided in her husband's blood, permanently. It still broke her heart, all these months later, to associate the word cancer with her husband, who to all intents and purposes appeared fit and healthy.

Josie had begun to cry as soon as she had begun to take in the terrible news. But not terrible news. She was trying to get her head around this disease that she had never heard of. Chronic Lymphocytic Leukaemia. The very phrase sounded terrifying. Like many, she associated leukaemia with children and the outcome was rarely positive from the little that she knew.

"So, there's no treatment?" She was struggling to understand how Mark could have cancer but not be treated for it. It was unthinkable. If anyone other than her best friend had told her this, she would have thought it a complete load of claptrap.

Maria shook her head. "It's mad isn't it? I couldn't believe it either. Sometimes I feel angry about it and other times I feel relieved. I wish there was just some... some, I don't know ... tablet or something that he could take. But then, I tell myself that if he doesn't need treatment, then it's not that serious. But how can fucking leukaemia not be serious?" She ended with a sob and Josie's heart broke into a thousand pieces for her friend, who had found love so late and now faced the possibility of losing it early. She knew that she had to force herself to be positive.

"I am so so sorry Maria. It's just awful. And I'm so so sorry that I haven't been there for you." She too was crying now. Being positive was not proving easy. She thought back to the events of the year and realised that Mark would have been shielding for much of it and then it must have been terrifying being back in the classroom, surrounded by teenagers. There had been so much controversy about whether schools should have re-opened in September and whether they should remain open for the entire term, whilst news abounded about the fact that teenagers were often asymptomatic but were passing it on to others, older and more vulnerable. The government had been adamant that the priority was protecting young people's mental health by keeping them in school and Josie could see both sides of the argument – the need for students to be learning within an educational setting and not isolated against the need to halt the spread of the virus - but now, hearing that her beloved friend's husband had been putting himself in even more danger than she had thought, made her feel angry at the lack of testing that had been offered to schools.

She did not know that just a couple of days later, the government was to perform yet another u turn, as on the thirtieth of December, they would put much of the country into tier four lockdown and delay the start of the new term for secondary school students. They would also announce the introduction of a mass testing regime for staff and students, due to start in the second week of term, with students home learning for the first week. But as she sat on the bench with Maria, she was filled with despair and fear. She reached across and stroked her friend's arm. She had no idea what she could possibly say that would not sound trite or patronising.

Chapter Thirty Five

2020 was seen out quietly, with no parties allowed and whilst people were pleased to see the end of what would be an historical year, with the virus mutating and quickening its pace, there seemed no end in sight. Josie had ordered a takeaway curry on New Year's Eve and had opened the Prosecco early on in the evening so before long she was dancing in the kitchen and revelling in the fact that she at least had her family around her. She had been quiet since learning about Mark's illness. She was so worried for her friend and her heart ached, hoping that Maria's optimism for the future would prove not to be misplaced. Harry had still not said what date he was due to return and Josie had buried the thought of him leaving again so didn't ask. He came into the kitchen and smiled at his mom dancing away to the radio, glass in hand. She threw her arms around him and dragged him into a bear hug.

"Love you, Harry!"

"I love you too ... look, mom. Can I tell you something?"

"Of course." Josie was suddenly still, alarm bells ringing. "What is it?" she asked, her voice full of concern.

Harry smiled. "Don't worry, it's nothing bad ... well, I don't think it is ... can we sit down a minute?"

They sat side by side at the kitchen counter and instinctively Josie took her son's hand.

He took a deep breath. "I have decided not to go back to Dubai."

Josie's heart leapt with happiness. She had had no idea how much she was dreading him going back.

"Oh thank god!" She pulled him close until he was laughing at the prospect of being smothered.

"But ... won't you get into trouble? Aren't you in a contract or something?" Josie was panicked, thinking about Brits ending up in Arabic jails.

Harry shook his head. "I was ... but I gave them proper notice before I came back. I'm sorry I haven't said anything, I felt like a failure but ... I was just so lonely ... it might have been different if we weren't going through the whole Covid thing but I knew that once I'd come home for Christmas I wouldn't be able to face going back. I did enjoy the work but it was so lonely in the evenings and weekends. Half term was awful. I wanted to come back so much. Especially when you were ill ..." His voice tailed off as he started to cry. "I'm sorry." He wiped his face, embarrassed. "I was so scared you know ... that ... that you might not make it ..."

Josie hugged her son. "Oh Harry, I'm so sorry. I wished you'd told me how you were feeling. You shouldn't have been going through this alone."

"I wanted you to be proud of me."

"Oh son, I am so proud of you."

"We both are." Neither of them had noticed that Trevor had come in quietly. He walked towards Harry and hugged him tight.

"Wow! This looks cosy. What's going on?"

They all turned as Hannah entered, bewildered.

"Come here." Trevor held out his arm to gather Hannah into the family hug. He had expected her to resist but as he drew her towards them he felt the tension, that he had not known was there, subside in his daughter. She was the first to pull away however.

"So what's going on?"

Harry filled her in and explained that he would be trying to get some temporary work, albeit unlikely, in the current circumstances. "But I've saved most of what I earned, so I won't need to sponge off anyone." He added hastily. "And then I've applied to do a PGCE at Birmingham uni so I can commute."

"Just when me and your mom were beginning to enjoy having our own space." Trevor raised his eyes to the ceiling but they all knew he was joking.

"Fair enough." Hannah looked pensive.

"You ok, love?" Josie looked at her daughter thoughtfully. "Hey, what are we doing, it's New Year's Eve, let's celebrate! Who wants a drink?

"Absolutely." Trevor realised he was a bit behind Josie, who had made a significant hole in the bottle of prosecco.

"I'll have a beer." Harry was visibly relieved to have unburdened himself and ready to let his hair down.

Hannah sighed. "Not for me, thanks."

"Really?" Josie really looked at her daughter now, seeing her pale face, circles under her eyes. "Are you ok? Do you feel ill?"

"I do actually." Hannah said quietly. "But I'm not … ill … I mean."

Josie and Trevor exchanged worried glances and Harry watched the scene unfold in front of him.

Hannah walked to the kitchen sink and poured herself a glass of water. She turned towards her parents and they both tried to read her expression. Was it defiance? Fear? What was going on?

"Hannah, love …"

"I'm pregnant"

Chapter Thirty Six

By the second weekend in January the Covid pandemic was at a record level of chaos, with hospitals under unprecedented risk of being unable to cope with the numbers that were being admitted on a daily basis. The UK had now recorded over 80,000 deaths since March, with daily death figures surpassing 1,000 on a number of the preceding days. The government's assurance that schools were safe and that parents should send their children to school on the first day of term was immediately followed on the evening of the first day back with the announcement of a third lockdown, with schools again closed to all but the most vulnerable children and the children of key workers. Like the rest of the country, Mark and Maria were incredulous at the number of U turns that had been made but both were relieved that he would now be required to shield again and therefore would not be putting himself in daily danger.

"It feels as though the world really has gone mad." Maria commented as they sat watching the news together. The week had seen riots and deaths at the United States Capitol building, with Donald Trump being accused of inciting violence from his supporters. "Our government might be incompetent, but they're not lunatics, thank god."

"You're right." Mark sighed. "I think I need a drink."

"Go on then." Maria didn't need much persuading but she was afraid of slipping into bad habits. She had been reading about how much people were eating and drinking and not exercising but it was pretty difficult to maintain healthy habits under the circumstances.

"Did you hear about those two women who were fined £200 for going for a walk outside of their local area?"

"It's ridiculous" Mark agreed. "They really need to get some perspective, we're all going to go insane." He handed her a glass of wine and took a sip of his own drink. "Heard from Josie lately?"

Maria gave him a strange look. Had he really just linked Josie to going insane?

"Sorry!" He clasped his hand to his mouth in horror. "I didn't mean …"

Maria laughed. "I know." She looked at her phone thoughtfully. "I have heard from her but … I don't know… her messages have been a bit … vague?"

"Why don't you give her a ring?"

"You trying to get rid of me?" Maria glanced at the TV.

"Well, I suppose if you wanted to go and have a girly catch up, I could watch the football for a bit?"

Maria whacked him playfully with a cushion. "I'll go and have a leisurely bath and give her a ring. But you will owe me! Find us a nice film!"

"Yeah right, I'll do my best." He had an unoptimistic tone. They had never watched so much television in the entire of their lives and were fast exhausting all avenues on that front.

Maria had had lots of lovely bath products for Christmas and lit a candle with the taunting name "Holiday Magic". God how she longed to escape somewhere hot and sunny.

She settled herself into a bath of bubbles, her wine glass on the side. She listened as Josie's phone rang out for a while and just as she thought it would go to voicemail, Josie picked up breathlessly.

"Sorry, I was just in the shower!"

"Ditto, well, I'm in the bath. Mark's watching yet more footy so thought we could have a catch up. How have you all been?"

Josie breathed deeply. Where to start? She might as well just take the bull by the horns.

"Hannah's pregnant!"

Maria was taken aback. She was not expecting that.

"Oh!" She was not quite sure what she should say … "And … that's … good? Not good?"

"Oh my god, Maria, I have no idea what has got into her."

Maria bit her tongue. It clearly wasn't the time for puns.

"So is she ... in a relationship?"

Josie had no idea how to respond to that question. Hannah had been very evasive about the nature of her relationship with the father of the baby she was adamant that she was keeping. She sighed as she answered her friend truthfully, "I really don't know. She says they became close and that she likes him but she hasn't even told him."

"And ... she definitely wants to go ahead with it?" Maria was shocked. This didn't sound like the Hannah she knew.

"She got really upset when I even hinted at the prospect of ... " Josie didn't like to say the word. It had brought back so many difficult memories. "Oh dear, Maria, I really don't know what to say to her. It's the last thing I expected. You know Hannah, she's always said she never wanted children. She seemed so intent on having a career, living her life ... you know?"

"I know." Maria answered understandingly. "But they haven't been able to live their lives have they? None of us has but think what it must have been like going to uni and not having that first crazy year. They were practically imprisoned from the word go so ... well ... it's not that surprising if you think about it ..."

"But why the hell would she want to keep it?" Josie heard herself sounding harsh but she was so upset by the idea that her daughter was about to wreck her future.

Maria was at a loss for words. She and Mark were eagerly awaiting the birth of their first grandchild but she understood that Hannah's situation was somewhat different.

"How many weeks is she?" They both knew that Maria was wondering if there was still time for Hannah to change her mind.

"About ten. But I can't encourage her either one way or the other can I?" Josie asked hopelessly. "She would hate me either way if she came to regret it. What a bloody mess."

"It has to be her decision, doesn't it, Jose? We both know that."

"I know." Josie's voice was sad.

"Look . . . even if she has the baby, which, to be honest, it sounds as though she has made up her mind ... it's not the end of the world. It works out for some people, you know. Lots of successful people started off on a rocky path. She can pick uni back up, still make a success of her life."

"I know but it all seems so unnecessary. She has years ahead to have babies... when she's settled ...

in a relationship ... in a bloody house of her own."
Josie snapped, hating the resentment in her voice.
"We had a massive row on New Year's Eve when
she told us. She said that if we didn't want her and
the baby at home, the council would find her
somewhere because they would be homeless. I
mean, for god's sake, as if I would throw her out ...
but ... "

"I know .... It's a lot for you to take on ... she
shouldn't just expect you to .... but that's what we
do isn't it?" Maria was full of sympathy; she was
aware that it was easy for her to say that that's
what parents do. As excited as she was about
becoming a grandparent, she was very conscious
that there would be a certain joy in being able to
hand the baby back and close her front door ... "I'm
so sorry, Josie."

Josie sighed. "We'll be ok, we'll just have to pull
together and count our blessings. But, everything
goes through my head, you know, I mean, what if
there's anything wrong with it? What if it turns out
to be one of these babies that needs 24/7 care?"

Maria laughed. "Come on Josie, don't they all?
Look, Hannah's young and the scans they do these
days are amazing. It's highly unlikely that she's
going to have anything other than a very healthy,
beautiful little baby. And ..." Maria forced
positivity into her voice and found that she was
actually feeling a hint of excitement at the
prospect. "We'll be grannies together! It'll be fun.
They will grow up together, like our kids did. We'll

have a new lease of life. And I'm sure that Hannah isn't going to just dump him or her on you all day and night. There's loads of support available, she'll probably be entitled to some free child care or something."

Josie had been entirely focused on all of the odds stacked against Hannah and why she shouldn't have this baby but talking to her friend made her realise that whatever happened a new life had been made by the daughter she loved and they would all love her son or daughter whatever the circumstances.

"Maria?" Josie's voice was weak.

"Yes?"

"I have to go. I think I need to go and give my daughter a hug and an apology."

Chapter Thirty Seven

By the end of January more than 100,000 people had died of Covid related deaths in the UK. It was a shocking figure and the whole country remained in full lockdown. Although more than six million people had received their first vaccine, the war was not yet won against the invisible killer. Outrageous stories in the news about Covid rule breakers were incredible to those who were compliant and literally thousands of people had been fined or criminally prosecuted for coronavirus-related offences. The final week of the month began with heavy snowfalls once again, meaning Josie and Trevor had missed their daily walk on several occasions. Josie was busy at work, albeit at home, and along with millions of others, was finding it hard to switch off without the daily commute. Sleepless nights had returned with a vengeance since Hannah's announcement and for many nights she had cried herself to sleep at the prospect of her daughter taking on a lifetime commitment at such a young age. The announcement on New Year's Eve had put paid to the dancing in the kitchen. Hannah had stubbornly refused to give them any further information regarding the father, other than saying that he was "a good friend". Josie had questioned how she could believe that from knowing someone barely three months but the question was pretty irrelevant, given that Hannah wasn't planning on involving him. This troubled Trevor considerably and he too shed tears but it was not for the same reason as Josie. They were sat in bed on a snowy Sunday morning. There was no rush to get up and their idle chatter returned to the topic of what they considered to be their daughter's plight.

"I can't stop thinking about the father. I imagine being in his shoes and having my child growing up without me even knowing they existed. It's not right. He has the right to know."

"I know." Josie agreed. "But how do we get that through to Hannah? You know how stubborn she is and the more we insist, the more stubborn she gets."

"We can't just give up though, can we? " Trevor persisted. "It's morally wrong. For the father and for the child."

"Let's sit her down and see if we can get through to her."

And so that afternoon, Trevor and Josie had broached the subject with their daughter.

"Hannah, love, " Josie had begun tentatively, "I know you have said that you don't want to involve the father but ..."

Hannah cut her off. "For Christ's sake, mother, we have had this discussion. It's my body, my business." It was the same line as she had trotted out on a number of occasions whenever Josie had dared to suggest that the father should be made aware. Hannah was surprised this time, however, because Trevor cleared his throat and began to speak.

"Hannah, it may be your body and yes, having the baby or not is ultimately your choice, as it should be, I mean no man should ever make that decision for a woman. However, if you are going to have a man's child, you have a moral obligation to let him know."

"Why do I?" Hannah interrupted hotly. "He didn't have sex with me to make a baby. It was an accident so effectively nothing to do with him. How can I be denying him something if he doesn't know it exists?"

It saddened Trevor to hear his daughter sounding so immature and selfish but he chose his words carefully, desperate not to pick a fight. He decided to take a different tack. He spoke softly.

"How would you feel, if you didn't know who your father was? If you were denied the chance to have a relationship with a second parent, who would potentially love you and give you experiences that you might otherwise be denied?"

"There is nothing that he could provide that I can't." Hannah stuck her chin out stubbornly.

"You're wrong, love." Trevor said gently. "This child deserves the right to know who their father is. And he has the right to know that he has a child on this earth."

"And what if he doesn't want to know?" Hannah contested.

"Is that what you think?" Trevor asked quietly.

Hannah shrugged and lowered her gaze.

"Is that what you're scared of? Rejection?"

For the first time since she had been home and, it seemed to Josie and Trevor, for many years, Hannah began to cry. Trevor hugged her. She was still his little girl and he wished he could make it all better for her. This bloody virus. He was convinced that there was absolutely no way she would consider having a baby if it wasn't for the events of the past year, which had turned everyone's lives upside down. She should be living the student life without a care in the world.

He sighed, she was not as tough as she liked to make out. "Look, Hannah. If you tell him and he doesn't want to know, then so be it and one day, if you're asked … when you're asked . . .you might have to hurt your child with that truth. But the damage that you will do to your relationship with your son or daughter when they find out that it was you who denied them a father, could be irreparable."

"You've said yourself that he's a good guy." Josie added. "He might be shocked, but I'm betting he would want to do the right thing."

Hannah looked at her mother, startled. "You're not talking about ... getting bloody married are you?"

Josie laughed. "Good god, Hannah, do you actually think I'm an idiot?"

Hannah raised her eyebrows.

"Ok, don't answer that." Josie waived her hands, dismissing the question. "But, what I'm talking about is . . . If he's a decent person, he will want to have some involvement in the child's life. And, well . . . we will help, of course we will, but believe me there will be times when you will be glad of the break and extra support."

Hannah was quiet. "He's a law student." She disclosed suddenly. It was the most that she had revealed about him.

"Ok . . .?" Trevor felt there was a point somewhere but he wasn't sure what it was.

"Wh . . . What if he wants custody of the baby or something and . . . and takes him from

me? Or her . . . "

"Oh Hannah, love. That's absolutely not going to happen. Your baby will be loved and looked after in a perfectly good home so no court would even entertain the idea." Josie was reminded of her daughter's youth and naivety and hastened to reassure her.

Trevor, ever the pragmatist, took the opportunity to present a slightly different perspective.

"Hannah, the only way that that could happen is if you persist in keeping the child to yourself and he finds out about him or her and chooses to fight you for custody." He reached for her hand. "Do the right thing, love, for everyone. We love you and will love your child and if it comes to it, that will be more than enough love but I bet there's a whole other family out there who will love it just as much. Please give your baby a chance to be loved by their father and grandparents, aunties ... uncles ... cousins ..."

Hannah pulled a face. "He's an only child, dad."

"Even better, think of the inheritance!"

Hannah allowed herself to smile, she knew that Trevor was joking. She rubbed her hands over her face. "Ok, I give in."

Hannah never gave in. Josie and Trevor exchanged a look and Trevor squeezed his daughter's hand. "We're here for you , love, whatever his response."

"I'll do it tomorrow."

Josie opened and closed her mouth. It was a win; tomorrow would be just great. She crossed everything that their daughter would get the support she deserved and that their grandchild would hopefully grow up feeling loved by both parents and their families.

Hannah took herself back upstairs and Trevor smiled in relief.

"Good work, Trevor." Josie knew that it was his words of wisdom that had swung it. If it had been just her and Hannah, it probably would have ended in world war three.

"I hope so," Trevor responded cautiously. "I hope I haven't just set her up for a hell of a fall."

* * *

The following day, Josie was busy with work but Trevor found it hard to settle to anything, worrying about the outcome of the conversation that Hannah was due to have with ....her "friend". Neither Hannah nor Harry was in the habit of rising early - there was nothing to get up for. Most of Hannah's lectures seemed to be in the afternoon, which didn't help to encourage her to get up at anything resembling what Trevor considered to be a respectable hour and so it was lunch time before he heard her descending the stairs. He tried to read her face as she came into the kitchen and poured herself a glass of water.

She took a seat next to him at the counter where he had been idly attempting the crossword from the previous day's paper. He put down his pen and waited for her to speak. Instinctively, he took her hand.

His daughter smiled. Trevor's heart skipped a beat. It felt like an eternity since he had seen her smile so genuinely.

"So ..... I told him....Will ... he's called Will ... " Hannah offered, unusually shy suddenly.

Trevor nodded gravely, every fibre of his being willing it to be good news. She looked so much happier ... but was that because she was going to get to have the baby to herself ....?

Josie walked in from the dining room, where during the day, she operated her "office". Trevor threw her a look which he hoped implied "Don't interrupt." She stood quietly and waited, her stomach in a thousand knots. Hannah looked at her mom and a small smile played on her lips.

"He was shocked." She began hesitantly, "We talk on snapchat most days so he couldn't believe that I'd kept it to myself. He was concerned ... about my studies ... and me not being able to do the things I'd talked about ... but he was ok with it." Hannah smiled properly now. "Yeah, actually, he was more than ok with it, he was really excited, started talking about us living together and being a proper family."

"I don't think you should rush into anything, love." Trevor was relieved to hear that his grandchild was going to have a father in their life but he was alarmed at the prospect of his daughter setting up home with someone she barely knew and they had not even met.

"I'm not stupid, dad." Hannah snapped but then immediately apologised. "I'm sorry. And ... and you were right ... thank you for making me do the right thing."

"Well .... We didn't make you." Josie interjected.

"No," Trevor added, eager to de-fuse any potential mother-daughter tension. "It was you ... you who chose to do the right thing." He added kindly.

"The thing is ..." Hannah had clearly now decided to be more open with them. "Well ... one of the things is ... as well as all the other stuff I said yesterday, "Well, the truth is ... I think his family are pretty much loaded .... I just didn't want it to look like I'd trapped him ... I'm still terrified that that's what his parents will think."

"Oh Hannah." Josie was at her daughter's side, "I wish you wouldn't bottle everything up ..." She gave her a hug. "Everything's going to be alright. This baby is going to be so so loved! It could be the best thing to come out of this bloody ridiculous year."

"Thanks mom!" Harry had slipped silently into the room, having hung around in the hallway long enough to come up to speed. "I came out remember!"

Chapter Thirty Eight

For Mark, February half term brought a welcome respite from the trials of remote teaching. Whilst some students did what they were asked on a daily and weekly basis, (in spite of difficulties presented by the sharing of and in some cases a complete lack of equipment within families, not to mention unreliable internet connections and the individual stresses within households), other students were unmotivated, disorganised or simply too distressed by the whole, repeated and protracted situation of trying to access learning without the physical presence of their teachers and the discipline of the classroom. There were those who thought that teachers were sitting around relishing "teaching from home" but anyone who had any real knowledge of what was going on would be well aware that the second school closure was a mental challenge for the professionals preparing the lessons as well as the young people who were exiled from education. Mark prided himself on having been able to keep up with the technological demands that had foisted themselves upon his position but it was the mental torture of knowing that many of the kids he cared about would be affected for ever by this gap in their expected school journey. Current Year 13 students had had the entire of their sixth form experience blighted by lockdowns and many of them would enter higher education having not sat a formal exam in over two years. Likewise, Year 11s would begin their post sixteen pathways having lost out on significant chunks of their last two vital years of compulsory schooling. Lower down the school, the term back in the classroom had seen many children resorting to what could only be described as feral behaviour as a result of an extended period of time at home with parents who couldn't or wouldn't enforce standards in manners and behaviour. Mark dreaded to think what the second return to the classroom would bring.

During his break, therefore, Mark and Maria managed to get out most days for a walk, in spite of unpredictable weather – the preceding week, that had seen sub zero temperatures, luckily gave way to an unseasonable rise to 12 or 13 degrees, albeit interspersed with wind and rain. Mark had a routine blood test to monitor his condition and he tried not to show any outward signs of anxiety during the twenty four hours' wait for the phone call which confirmed his results. Maria sat by his side and listened as the consultant reeled off figures which, to their collective relief, indicated that his CLL was stable. Maria kissed the top of Mark's head. It was almost a year since his diagnosis and although Maria sometimes awoke in the middle of the night, terrified that she would be left alone, she generally managed to convince herself that they could continue to look forward to their lives as much as anyone else.

By the end of the week off, they heard that 17.5 million people had received their first vaccine but some 120,000 had now died and each week there were shocking stories that indicated that it was no longer just the elderly and vulnerable that were being taken prematurely by the indiscriminate virus.

"But the numbers in hospital are now falling daily." Mark tried to reassure Maria when she voiced her fears, not for the first time.

"I just want our lives back." Maria mused sadly. "I know it's selfish; we are so lucky compared to some ..." Her voice trailed off.

"Come on, stay positive, let's google some holidays and start planning ahead. I am sure that by the summer, we will be getting back to some kind of normality."

Maria shook herself. "I'm sorry, you're right. Not to mention that we will be busy being grandparents!"

A couple of weeks later, Maria's long awaited grandchild put in an appearance. Molly and Dan had decided to buck the trend and not find out the sex of their baby. Maria had been dying to find out but perfectly understood their desire not to fall for the "Reveal Party" culture and all that nonsense. Molly hadn't even had a baby shower, saying that it was embarrassing expecting friends and family to fork out for gifts for their baby before it was even born.

It was the day before the national return to school and Mark had been preparing for the return of students to his classroom. Again, he should have been shielding but he simply couldn't bring himself to stay at home and not do his job. He felt reassured that his vaccine would have kicked in by now and although not a 100 percent guarantee, he felt better armed than he had been previously. The weather had been sunny and bright and they had had a Sunday stroll around a local nature reserve, which, albeit packed with like minded couples and families with limited leisure options, was a pleasant change from the four walls. Maria was in the kitchen, preparing their evening meal and listening to the radio. Her ears pricked at the sound of Mark's mobile and she picked up straight away on his excited but cautious tone.

As she entered the living room, she heard him saying "So everything's ok? They're both all right?"

Maria was at his side immediately, craning her neck so that she too could hear Dan's breathless announcement.

"Mia Louise" He stated proudly.

"Oh my god, I knew it!" shouted Maria. "A girl! I'm so happy!"

Dan filled them in on a few details, weight, times and so on and assured them that all was ok. "We'll most probably be home later on."

Maria bit her tongue, desperate to find out when they could visit. Lockdown was still lockdown and they were still not allowed in each other's homes.

"We'll do a WhatsApp call as soon as, I promise." Dan assured them both, "and the weather's improving, we'll find a way to see you outside as soon as we can."

"Don't worry about us," Maria responded, quashing her disappointment at not being able to rush around to hold their new grandchild and of course help the new parents. "As long as you're all ok."

Once they'd said their goodbyes, however, Maria buried her head in Mark's chest. "It's so unfair, I just want us to all be together."

"We shall be." Mark too was disappointed that Covid created such a barrier to what should have been a joyous occasion. "We just have to follow the rules and be patient for a while longer."

He kissed the top of Maria's head. "Doesn't stop us celebrating though, Nanny Maria."

Maria smiled self-consciously, not quite sure how she felt about that title. Moments later, Mark was popping a cork in the bottle of Champagne that he had had in the fridge, awaiting the safe arrival of his grandchild.

"School tomorrow!" Maria wagged a finger.

"I think I'll manage."

They clinked glasses "To Mia Louise."

"And the future." Added Mark.

Chapter Thirty Nine

Gradually, spring arrived in fits and spurts, with the weather as unpredictable as ever from one day to the next. By the end of February Boris had delivered his "roadmap out of lockdown, which was slower than many would have preferred but after the disastrous second wave, the government was clearly erring on the side of caution. Schools re-opened on the 8th of March and those in care homes could have one regular visitor. By Easter, seven people or two households were allowed to meet outside. Tennis, open air sports and open air swimming pools were allowed to re-open but the re-opening of hairdressers, gyms and beer gardens did not take place until the 12th of April. Life was only slowly returning to normal, with outside table service only, which meant that social gatherings were pretty much dependent on the weather. Josie was nervous on the afternoon that Harry went out for the first time in what seemed an eternity. Erin knocked the door and waited for him outside; she waved to Josie who came forward hurriedly, remembering just in time that they were still not allowed to hug. She had waved them off with a mixture of sadness for a future that might have been but happiness for the future that she felt certain held so much for her son, with his positive mindset and kind nature complementing his academic abilities.

Josie had begun to spend more time with her daughter, who, on the whole remained up-beat and excited for the new chapter that she had started. They had met Will a couple of times, meeting to eat outdoors at a local pub. Josie had been reassured by the clear affection that he had for Hannah. He was old-fashioned in his chivalry but clearly forward-thinking as he spoke brightly of their future together. Whilst it was clear that he came from a family with money, it was also obvious that he was hugely ambitious and intended to make his own way in the world. He also spoke encouragingly of how they could ensure that Hannah had the opportunity to return to her studies as soon as she wished to. Josie could not imagine Hannah as a stay-at-home mother in spite of her newly discovered maternal instincts. They had had fun shopping for baby equipment and clothes and it had been agreed that, for the first few months at least, Hannah would stay at home so as to have her own mother's support. Will was happy with this as it had been made clear that he too was welcome to stay.

As the weeks went by, it became clear that Harry had met someone and Josie and Trevor had encouraged him to bring him home to meet them but as yet Harry was keeping him to himself. He had shown them pictures and Josie had giggled at the sight of the handsome young man smiling at the camera. "You have good taste, son!" she had commented, glancing at her husband, who she was relieved to see was smiling good-naturedly. Harry still saw a lot of Erin and Josie knew how hard it was for Trevor to let go of his dreams but she knew for sure now that Harry had his father's full support and whatever his future family looked like, Trevor would be there putting shelves up and offering paternal advice just as if his son had been born heterosexual.

And so spring became summer, with uncertain weather, heat waves one week and down pours the next. Covid remained a daily news item, with concerns over new strains and the uncertainty of travel restrictions, self isolating, quarantining and the requirement for tests before travel either in or out of the country. Josie, along with the rest of the country, was weary of it all and wondered when, if ever, life would truly return to normal.

Chapter Forty

It had been a beautiful, sun-filled weekend. Maria's birthday present to Josie had been an-overnight spa break. It was originally planned for the end of June but this had had to be postponed due to the delay in relaxing the lockdown rules, which had been planned for the twenty first of June but had been pushed back to nineteenth of July due to the latest strain of the disease. The irony of the spa break had not been lost on Josie and she had hugged her friend sheepishly, not wanting to think of the previous year's disastrous date with Jeff. She had looked tentatively at Trevor.

"It's all sorted," Maria had reassured her, eager for there not to be any awkwardness. "We have Trev's permission!"

Trevor had laughed, also keen not to rake up unwelcome memories. "Yeah, well, I'll hold the fort." He offered magnanimously.

"Humph!" Jodie had responded with mock objection. "You mean you'll have a wonderful day and night watching non-stop sport!"

"The thought had not crossed my mind!"

And so, Maria had insisted on driving, as it was her treat for her friend. "It's no big deal, we can both have a drink anyway if we're staying over."

Josie had been concerned about sharing a car and a room. However, in spite of ongoing and seemingly prolific cases, in all honesty, even Maria had relaxed her approach.

"We cannot continue to put our lives on hold" she had asserted, "The whole point of us getting double jabbed was so that we can return to normal. Most people now are just getting cold symptoms so I don't get the big deal."

Josie was pleased that her friend had overcome her terrible anxiety that something awful would happen to Mark and was just pleased that at last she had the chance to spend some quality time relaxing with her friend. For both of them, it seemed an absolute age since they had had anything resembling a pamper day other than within the confines of their own homes and they both knew the limitations of that. Even with grown up kids, there was always one of them who would have something urgent they needed that they just couldn't sort themselves the minute those face masks went on or their feet had just been nicely wrapped.

Having checked in at the spa, which was tranquil and pristine, they had begun with a work out in the gym, which left them both feeling the effects of a year of limited exercise and un-reluctantly they had given in and devoted the remainder of the day to lazing around the pools, the Jacuzzis, saunas and a very lazy lunch. After lunch they each had two treatments booked and by the time they met up again, the afternoon was slipping into evening.

"Oh Maria, it's been a lovely day, thank you so much."

They were indulging in a second bottle of prosecco and the meal that they had been served was divine.

"So much lost time." Maria mused. "I intend to spend the rest of my life making up for it, that's for sure." She chinked her glass against her friend's. "Let's hope we never have to go through anything like that year again."

"Absolutely," agreed Josie. "Year and a half more like. I can't believe that it is still going on. I am sick of hearing about it to be honest with you and just hope we get to go on our river cruise. We have so much to look forward to." She smiled happily, thinking of Hannah's baby due before the summer was over. "Can't wait until we're pushing prams together again!"

"Absolutely." Maria agreed, " I'm so envious of you going on that cruise!"

"I have been totally spoiled." Josie admitted. She sighed contentedly. "You know ... I do regret being such an idiot with the whole bloody Jeff thing ... but ... I can't help feeling glad that it's brought me and Trev so much closer."

"All's well, that ends well." Maria smiled affectionately.

They moved away from the restaurant and settled themselves into a lavish sofa next to a gently babbling water feature.

"So nice to be away from the TV!"

"Tell me about it, I spent a whole year watching utter drivel. I am convinced I became addicted ... I've never really been that bothered but I would binge watch one rubbish series after another!"

"I know and we used to wake up and start talking about what we would have for dinner because there was simply nothing else to look forward to!"

"Nightmare!" Maria shuddered, remembering some of the darkest days of lockdown number three when the weather was freezing and every day felt like groundhog day, with constant press conferences and stories about the rule breakers, arguments about the R rate and whether schools should be open . . . "I don't want this evening to end, it's been so lovely."

"Me neither. I am so full though, I could do with getting back in that gym!"

"We can have another session in the morning. However, my dear, for now ... I think we should sample those delicious sounding cocktails!"

Several cocktails later, they teetered on their heels, unaccustomed now and unsteady on their feet, they giggled their way to their room and collapsed into giggles on their twin beds, not even remembering what they were laughing about.

"Oh dear, Jose," Maria slapped a hand over her face, "Ish your bed spinning?" she slurred.

Josie, somehow, felt marginally more sober than her friend appeared to be. She pulled off her own heels and then set about pulling off her friend's

"I'll get us some water."

"Fanks." Maria hiccupped and then giggled before hiccupping again loudly.

By the time Josie returned from the mini-bar and precariously poured two glasses of water, Maria was snoring.

Josie set the glasses down and looked at her friend. She was suddenly consumed with laughter as she remembered the sorry state of Jeff, lying dribbling on the bed. Her laughter, however, gave way to sobs as the trauma of the past year or so came bubbling back up and consumed her drunken thoughts.

"Pull yourself together, Josie Winters." She admonished herself sternly as she gazed at her reflection in the bathroom mirror, somewhat blurred by the effect of the alcohol. She had a little conversation with herself as she cleansed her face, reminding herself of how lucky they were to have come through the pandemic relatively unscathed. She thought of how much they had to look forward to – the thought of holding Hannah's baby in her arms always left her weak with longing – and she hoped that the river cruise would be the much needed escape from reality that she needed. She pushed away the nagging doubt about amber list countries and red list countries and forced herself to remain optimistic. She felt blessed as she thought sadly of the burden that Maria and Mark carried each day, watching and waiting, hoping that they too would get to enjoy their grandchildren, holidays and a long retirement …

She sat gently on her friend's bed and carefully wiped away Maria's make up, knowing how dreadful she would feel if she awoke and felt her pores clogged by foundation after all that earlier pampering. Maria stirred as Josie smoothed moisturiser into her skin and Josie soothed her and reminded her to drink plenty of water.

"Fanks, Jose, love you mate!"

Josie smiled and kissed Maria's head. "I love you too. Sleep tight."

Josie had not expected to sleep so well, being in an unfamiliar bed and away from Trevor. She cringed inwardly as she remembered the nights when she and Trevor had slept in separate rooms and then he had left whilst she had Covid. How afraid she had been that they would never be together again. She pulled the cool, cotton sheets around her and fell into a deep and blissful sleep.

It was already after nine when she awoke. She could see that Maria had changed position and had obviously drunk most of the glass of water, which was a good sign. Josie pulled on the soft, complementary robe. Their ground floor room opened up on to a small terrace overlooking extensive grounds and a lake, which shimmered now in the morning sunshine. Josie stepped out on to the terrace and breathed in the fresh, clear air. Her head felt surprisingly clear. She looked back towards her friend and hoped that she too had benefitted from a good night's sleep. Josie took a seat and pulled out her mobile phone.

Trevor's phone rang out for a while and Josie was just expecting it to switch to answerphone, when he answered, somewhat breathlessly.

"Hey" Josie laughed, "What are you up to?"

"Well ..." Trev's tone was sheepish. "I might have forgotten to water your baskets last night, so was just catching up."

Josie laughed. Was that all she had to worry about? She filled him in on their evening and half listened whilst he told her the football scores.

"How's Hannah?" Josie was always worrying about her daughter, especially now that she was in her final trimester. "And Harry, of course? Is everything ok?"

"Everything is fine. Enjoy the rest of your day. Don't get rushing back on our account. We're grown ups remember! You'll soon have your hands full again when Baby Winters arrives!"

"Er, how do you know it's going to be a Winters?"

"Good point." Trevor conceded "But it will be a Winters in his or her heart"

"If our grandchild has your heart, they'll be a good un."

"Thank you. Love you Josie."

"I love you too. See you later!"

Josie could hear Maria murmuring and she walked back into the room to find her swinging her legs out of bed.

"Ouch!" Maria was rubbing her head. "I didn't realise I was so out of practice. How are you so ... so okay?"

Josie laughed. "Take these." She offered her a couple of paracetamol and re-filled her glass. "Come on, let's go and have some breakfast .... soak up the alcohol."

Breakfast was a sumptuous buffet of fruits, fresh juices, yogurts and a wide selection of hot and cold dishes. Josie discovered that she was surprisingly ravenous and tucked in heartily.

"Sorry, " apologised Maria, "I can't face food at the moment." She pushed a piece of melon around her plate but managed to empty a cafetiere of strong, black coffee.

"Are you going to be ok? Do you need me to get you anything?"

"No, don't worry, I feel great after that coffee." Maria assured her.

"I can't face the gym but let's go back into the spa and sit in the jacuzzi for a bit. If that's ok with you?"

Maria appeared to recover once she got in the water, the smell of the chlorine awakening her senses. "God, Josie, I think we should do this more often. I need to build my alcohol tolerance back up!"

"Absolutely!" Josie agreed, readily. She was looking forward to being a grandparent but she was well aware that she was now the parent of two grown up children and told herself that she deserved to start having a bit more "me time."

"Where have the years gone?" Maria sighed as she relaxed back into the bubbles.

"Crazy isn't it?"

"We've had some good times though." Maria mused wistfully.

"We have indeed. I was looking at some photos the other day. Do you remember when we all went to that Greek Island together?"

"Oh I do. Do you remember when we sat by the harbour and that lorry just literally fell over and into the sea?!"

"Oh god, that was so funny, the Greeks just shrugged their shoulders and carried on with their breakfasts!"

"Imagine if there'd been the internet in those days!"

"Thank god there wasn't!"

"Well yes, true, people don't half get themselves into some scrapes these days."

The morning passed by at a leisurely pace, filled with idle chatter and laughter. All too soon, they were checking out.

"Thank you so much Maria, it's been bliss." Josie smiled as they strolled into the bright sunshine of the afternoon. "Are you feeling ok to drive, by the way?"

Maria waved off her thanks and her concern.

"All is fine. And we will definitely do this again soon."

Maria connected her Bluetooth to the car media system and soon they were singing along to "Summer of 69"

Josie sighed as the song came to an end and glanced at her friend. "Can't wait until we get to go to concerts again. It's unbelievable how many things we still have to do that were postponed."

Maria reached over to her friend and squeezed her arm gently. "We will have our dancing shoes on again, girl, don't worry."

"Eighteen 'til I die" blared out loudly, summing up their youthful spirit to perfection. They exchanged a warm smile that lingered a split second too long. A second that Maria would regret for the rest of her life.

The flash of a red car came hurtling towards them out of nowhere, taking the bend wide, Maria had no time to swerve and there was nowhere to go in the narrow lane. All Maria remembered was a blood curdling scream and what sounded like an explosion.

Chapter Forty One

Trevor had mown and strimmed the lawns and was busy pulling weeds out of the front border. He looked up and saw the police car heading down the road. "About time." He muttered to himself. Since their burglary last year, he had been hyper alert to the number of strange cars/vans that seemed to check out the neighbourhood on a regular basis and he was acutely aware of the limited police patrols, which irked him, given the considerable council tax that they paid. He pulled at a stubborn weed and wiped his forehead with the back of his hand, straightening slowly as he realised that the police car was slowing as it approached. "Sat Nav probably got them lost again, shouldn't wonder." Trevor said to himself, preparing to give directions. He nodded politely at the young female police officer who glanced in his direction before turning off the ignition and making a comment to her colleague. The pair of them looked like they should still be in sixth form, Trevor reflected wryly.

"Mr Winters? Trevor Winters?"

Trevor was jolted from his thoughts at the sound of his own name. He was still crouched over the border of summer plants, but rocked back on his heels now, dusting soil from his thighs with several flicks of his hands. Suddenly, he was consumed with panic and pushed himself unsteadily to a standing position. Like every parent, this was a scene that he had played out in his mind many times when Harry and Hannah had been out with friends who had newly passed their driving test. But Harry and Hannah were inside. Safe. Which could only mean …

"Josie …" his wife's name barely left his lips as the colour drained from his cheeks.

"Sir," the young PC ventured softly, "I am PC Holsworth and this is my colleague PC Anderson. Can we step inside?

But Trevor was rooted to the step. He didn't hear the front door open or see Hannah and Harry cross the lawn.

When, later, he would try to remember these moments, Trevor didn't recall the words that were exchanged and he was unaware of going into the house. All he could recall was a howl which began in his stomach, rendering his legs lifeless and immobile, and came bubbling upwards, ripping through his heart.

He was sat on the sofa, Hannah and Harry either side of him. They were all gripping hands and Hannah's free hand guarded her swollen belly.

"It was instant. She wouldn't have felt a thing." PC Holloway was saying quietly. Trevor felt as though he were in a vacuum, the police officer's voice was echoing around him. He felt a drowning sensation but conscious of his children beside him, he tried to find some paternal force that would render him useful, supportive and strong for their sakes but he was lost, overcome with shock, grief, disbelief. He felt their numbness, their silence filling the room.

It was Harry who finally found the strength to speak.

"What about Maria?" His voice was hesitant.

P C Holsworth released her lips from the grim line they had formed as she had allowed the news to sink in. It was not the first time that she had had to perform this unthinkable task but nothing would ever make it easier. "She's in hospital. I'm not entirely sure of the extent of her injuries but she is stable."

They all nodded. Maria was like part of their family. Another fatality would be more than they could bear and yet each of them wondered whether they were the only one to question the injustice, the unfairness, the luck of the draw. Why did it have to be Josie ...

In the meantime, Mark had received a phone call from the hospital. He was shaking as he brought his car to life on the drive. His mind was an explosion of unanswered questions. What had happened? How serious was it? What about Josie? The conversation with the hospital had been brief. He had been too shocked to formulate logical thoughts let alone questions.

Mark was a confident driver and yet hearing the news that his wife had been involved in a car accident made him question every decision he made, so the fifteen minute drive to the hospital seemed like an eternity and although in reality he was at Maria's side within a further ten minutes of parking his car, his patience as he waited his turn at the hospital reception was fragile. He had an overwhelming sense of needing to shout out – surely no one else's need could be more urgent that his right now?

The nurse who led him to his wife was efficient but empathetic and filled him in on the details, as much as she knew at least. There had been a collision. Both of Maria's legs were broken and she had a neck injury but none of her injuries was life-threatening. "She is just going to need a lot of TLC for a while." The nurse commented, glancing at her notes and frowning distractedly.

Mark had been filled with a sense of relief. Maria would be pretty exasperated with two broken legs but thank god, she would be okay. As he watched the kindly nurse reading through the notes on the clipboard, however, his relief was short-lived. He sensed that there was more and that it wasn't good …

"Can I call you Mark?"

"Of course, what is it? What aren't you telling me?"

The nurse led him into a side room. "Mark, please. Take a seat for a moment, I need to run through a few extra details."

Mark perched uneasily on the plastic chair. His palms were sweaty, his legs weakened with worry.

"The lady that your wife was travelling with ... "

"Josie, " Mark answered breathlessly. "Is ... is she ok .... Is she here?"

He watched the nurse's face, solemn and sympathetic, "They were friends?"

Mark heard the past tense. He covered his face with his hands. Jesus Christ, no, this could not be happening. He shook his head and he felt the tears spilling on to his hands.

"I'm so sorry, Mark."

"I don't understand ... what the hell happened?"

"I don't know the details, I'm sorry. There was another vehicle but I'm afraid that's all I know."

Mark was not to know that that was not all she knew. She knew that the driver of the other vehicle had also been brought in, shortly after Maria. She had no idea who, if anyone, had been at fault but protocol and common sense meant that there was no way that she could divulge this information to the bereaved and heartbroken friends of a fifty year old woman.

Mark ran a hand through his hair, his brain was heavy, he couldn't think straight.

"Does she know? Does Maria know?"

"No, she's been sedated. You can see her briefly but she will need to rest. I would suggest that we give it a day or so before we break the news ..."

Chapter Forty Two

It was a grey, August morning, almost as though the sun did not have the audacity to shine. Maria, still wheel-chair bound and her neck held by a brace, sat silent and pale in the crematorium. Mark too was ashen, his suit hung loosely, indicating recent, involuntary weight loss. Trevor sat, hands linked with his daughter on one side and his son on the other. His face firmly set, steeling himself against the temptation to give into the grief that continued to rip through his heart. Hannah, heavily pregnant, was uncomfortable and hot and was grateful for the presence of Will, who helped her to stay calm and focused rather than give into the anger at the unfairness of death that had stolen her mother when she needed her most. Harry tentatively reached out on his other side and the handsome, young man that he had become so close to and who had helped him remain sane in the past, heart-breaking weeks, squeezed his hand back, indicating that he was there for him.

Trevor had insisted that Mark, Maria and their family be included as part of the family, saying their final respects to Josie and they sat in front of Josie's extended family, friends, neighbours and colleagues. Whilst restrictions on numbers had been lifted, it was still advised that people attending funerals socially distanced, wore masks and avoided singing. Maria recalled the times when they had occasionally joked about their own send offs, imagining it a joyous affair at the end of a long and fulfilled life. Tears rolled down her cheeks uncontrollably and Mark wondered if she would ever forgive herself as they had all forgiven her. The verdict had been clear. The driver of the other vehicle was three times over the legal limit for alcohol. He had been on the wrong side of the road. Maria, whilst there was alcohol in her system, was under the limit and the police had been emphatic that no blame lay at her door. Trevor had attempted to convince her that the boot could easily have been on the other foot, but the fact remained that it was not. Maria was alive and Josie wasn't.

It was a short service. Trevor, Hannah and Harry had agreed that they would not be able to keep it together well enough to make a speech and so each of them shared their memories for the funeral celebrant to deliver a speech that had been put together based on their loving and happy memories. She was a gentle lady, in her fifties and she spoke warmly of Josie, who in life had been a loving, caring, attentive mother of two children who adored her. She was loved, un-waveringly by her husband and she was a life-long friend to Maria. At Trevor's request, they listened to Celine Dion's "My heart will go on" and each of them allowed the tears to fall freely, drowning in their own sorrow but somehow believing that their hearts would in fact go on and knowing that Josie would stay there for ever.

About the Author

Lainy J. Thomas is a teacher who also writes fictional family drama. She lives in Staffordshire, England with her husband and her imagination. She has two grown up sons, a step-son, two step-daughters and so far two adorable grandchildren.

If you enjoyed, "Just one Year", please review!

Also available on Amazon:

A Place Called Home

Father Things and Flings

https://www.amazon.co.uk/stores/Lainy-J.-Thomas/author/B008ODBJQY?ref=dbs_a_mng_rw t_scns_share&isDramIntegrated=true&shoppingPo rtalEnabled=true

Printed in Great Britain
by Amazon